SAM CRESCENT & STACEY ESPINO

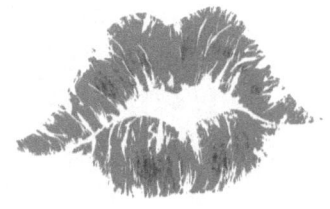

EVERNIGHT PUBLISHING ®

www.evernightpublishing.com

SAM CRESCENT & STACEY ESPINO

HARD TO GET

Killer of Kings, 4

Sam Crescent and Stacey Espino

Copyright © 2017

Chapter One

Riley carried the small bag of garbage to the curb and tossed it in the metal can. Just like clockwork, her neighbor, Mr. Tall, Dark, and Mysterious, did the same. She waved to him, and, as usual, he ignored her and walked back along the path to his house.

What an asshole, she thought. *A fucking sexy asshole, but still.*

She'd bought the tiny bungalow almost a year and a half ago, thanks to a government subsidy program and a shitload of bank loans. Her other neighbors seemed friendly enough—it was the suburbs after all. It was just *him.* She knew absolutely nothing about her next-door neighbor, not even a name. None of her attempts at making contact had any success, but at least it wasn't just her. The man was reclusive, choosing to keep to himself, avoiding just about everyone.

Riley had conjured up all kinds of exciting scenarios in her head. A few months ago, she'd convinced herself he was running an illegal drug lab. She'd crept along the bushes after he left one day and peeked in a crack of the curtains through the front window. It was disappointing to find a very normal looking living room, one she'd expect to see on the cover of a boring home and garden magazine. So, she was back to square one, wondering who the mysterious man really was.

She returned to the house to collect her purse and car keys, and then made the drive to work. It was only fifteen minutes away in a small outdoor plaza. Riley had put absolutely everything—blood, sweat, tears, and her last penny—into starting up her own bakery. It was a small half-unit, and she couldn't afford any staff yet, but it was hers. She'd stop at nothing to make it a success.

"Morning, Riley."

She waved to Janet, one of the insurance agents who worked a couple doors down. Riley knew most of the people in the plaza, from owners to staff, but she wouldn't call any of them close friends. She preferred her privacy, and she'd been fiercely independent since she could remember. It was too much risk to invest in people who would inevitably let her down, not unlike her own mother and just about every guy she'd ever dated. Her best bet was to focus on herself, her bakery, and the fact she didn't need another person to make her feel whole.

After she unlocked the glass door and flipped the closed sign to open, she turned on the lights and made her way behind the counter. Today, she had a wedding cake to prepare, two birthday cakes, and she had to start her usual offerings of bread, buns, and cookies. She loved baking and creating something from simple ingredients. It was her personal escape, her therapy. If she was upset, she could lose herself in the process; if she was angry, she could beat the dough. Mostly, baking made her happy, giving her purpose in an otherwise fucked up life.

"Hey," said Janet, slipping in the front door.

"What's up?"

"Did you hear they rented out the corner unit?"

The largest unit in the plaza had been vacant for over six months. Since it was supposed to be the anchor store for their plaza, everyone was anxious for it to get a tenant. "Really? By who?"

She rolled her eyes. "A bar. Can you believe it?"

Riley shrugged. "A lot of plazas have bars."

"Yeah, but they're busy *after* hours, when we're both closed. I can't see how it'll be a benefit."

"Nothing we can do about it." She washed her hands and then began reaching for her mixing bowls on the higher shelves. "I'm used to relying on myself, anyway."

She'd never gotten any breaks in her life, so she wasn't going to count on any now. Yes, she prayed for business to pick up, but she wasn't going to hold her breath.

"I can see that. I can't believe you run this place all by yourself." Janet absently flipped through the cake book on the counter.

"Well, I'm not exactly busy enough to hire help. Even if I was, I couldn't afford it."

Janet looked at her watch. "I better go. I have a client coming in ten minutes."

Once Riley was alone, she lost herself in her work, the scent of flour and cinnamon calming her nerves. As much as she chose not to dwell on it, the bottom line was always in the back of her mind. If her store went out of business, she would lose everything, including her house. She'd be able to get another job, but that wouldn't change the fact she owed the bank a small fortune.

She was used to surviving, but it wasn't easy with one fickle income. All her neighbors were married, many with children—except her next-door neighbor. She'd never seen a woman come or go, no visitors either. Now that her thoughts drifted to her mystery man, her anxiety eased and her body heated up. How could he have such an effect on her, especially when they hadn't shared two words?

Her childhood obsession with Nancy Drew books fueled her curiosity. He was a mystery she wanted to unravel. Was he an accountant? A secret agent? The guy was tall and always wore layers of black, even in the heat. Maybe a bodyguard?

She chuckled to herself as she put the first dough ball into a greased pan. Reading made life tolerable and her fictional love life more exciting. If only the heroes in her romance novels were real. Even if they were, they always went for the picture-perfect damsels in distress, and Riley had never been a beauty pageant contender—and she didn't need to be saved.

The door bells chimed as two women came into her shop mid conversation. She recognized them from her neighborhood.

"Oh, it's you … sorry, I don't remember your name," said the blonde.

"Riley."

"Right, you live near the end of the block. I didn't know you worked here. I'm Amanda, and Karen lives across the road from me."

Riley smiled, brushing her hands over her apron to remove the excess flour. "It's nice to meet you both. Can I help you with anything?"

Amanda looked at her friend before facing Riley again. "I'm having a block party this weekend for my tenth anniversary. I need a large cake, a hundred rolls, and some fancy treats," she said. "You did get an invitation, didn't you?"

She shook her head. It wasn't a surprise. Riley

didn't exactly fit into the social circles of their urban-chic suburb. At twenty-eight she was younger than most in the neighborhood. Her naturally black hair had a few streaks of blue that always seemed to turn heads. She liked to be unique, embracing her creative side, and not caring what anyone else thought.

"It must have gotten lost in the mail." Amanda tittered. Did she realize how transparent she was? Riley had always been a good judge of character, and these women were too shallow for her liking. "Karen, do you have any more invitations?"

Karen rooted around in her purse and then handed her a small white and gold envelope.

"Thank you," Riley said, pocketing the invitation. She pulled out her notepad. "Let me get your order down before I forget."

By the time she closed up for the evening, she was beat. Amanda expected a lot with only two days' notice. Normally, Riley would refuse such a tight turnaround, but she wasn't about to refuse a big order like that.

She drove home, listening to her favorite radio station with the windows open. Riley loved the longer days of summer. As she turned onto her street, she noticed her neighbor pulling out of his driveway. The craziest thought popped in her head. She tried to push it away, convincing herself only crazy stalkers followed people. But this was her chance to feed her curiosity. She'd only follow for a little while, no harm done.

Riley bit her lip as she passed her house, following a good distance behind her neighbor's black SUV. When they got on the freeway, heading towards the city, she began to curse herself for being so stupid. Every time she decided to get off at the next exit, she argued with her conscience that she'd come this far and had to follow it through. The guy drove like a fucking maniac, weaving in and out of traffic, well above the posted speed limit. When he finally pulled off at an exit, she was relieved that they hadn't traveled too far.

She stayed a safe distance behind. If he noticed her following, she'd have to face him every day of her life. It would be a disaster. He stopped at some sort of sports complex or community center, parking around back. She did the same a few minutes later. It was a sketchy neighborhood, with graffiti on just about every wall or dumpster. Riley swallowed hard as she exited her car. She could smell weed coming from a group of men behind the building, so she scurried down the path to the front as fast as she could without attracting attention.

Riley entered the large foyer of a bustling open gym, a boxing ring in the distance, and a lot of guys working out. The mix of pounding bass, metal clanging, and shouting left her in a daze as she tried to spot the mystery man through the glass wall.

"Can I help you?"

She turned around after hearing the deep voice, coming face to face with a severe scowl. The pissed-off man wore just shorts, boxing tape on his hands. Now that she took notice, there were nearly a dozen sketchy guys covered in ink loitering around the entrance. Riley was not prepared for this. A couple more men approached her, and she froze. She had no reason to be there, and suddenly wished she had just pulled into her driveway like she did every day after work.

Damn you, Nancy Drew!

"You don't belong here," said the man.

"I was just looking for someone."

He crossed his arms over his chest as the other men surrounded her. "What's his name?"

She couldn't answer. Not only did she not know

her neighbor's name, but she'd suddenly lost her ability to speak.

"Maybe she came looking for a good time," said another man from behind her.

"I don't mind some extra cushion for the pushin'."

Riley remembered the knife she always carried in her purse. She pulled back the zipper and began to casually root through all her junk. The asshole in front of her snatched her bag and tossed it to his friend.

"Hey!" she shouted.

She was too caged in to run or try to get her purse back. Her adrenaline spike made her dizzy. Why did her neighbor come here, to one of the worst areas of the city? It was riddled with gangs. There were stabbings and shootings reported every night on the evening news.

All of a sudden, the whole group of men backed away from her as if she was on fire. Their looks of malice were replaced with submissiveness. It didn't make sense.

"Why are you following me?"

Riley whirled around, nearly toppling over when she saw her next-door neighbor standing at the entrance. He was even taller up close, well over six feet, his shoulders massive. His dark eyes held no hint of emotion, just the same blank slate she'd seen time and time again.

"I w-wasn't," she stuttered. Her fear morphed into a heady embarrassment. She looked like Ms. Desperado or maybe he thought she was a psychopath.

He had a black gym bag slung over one shoulder. When he jutted his chin, the man who'd taken her bag rushed to hand it back to her. She held it against her chest like a life preserver.

"This is a bad neighborhood," he said. "Not a place for little girls." He pointed a finger to the gym, and all the men who'd harassed her fought to get through the double glass doors, leaving them alone.

Why did they listen to him? Why were they afraid?

Up close, she guessed he was in his early forties, but fuck he looked good. The rush of adrenaline, plus being so close to the object of her obsession, made her pussy pulse with need.

"I was just leaving," she said.

"Be smart. Keep to the suburbs."

She walked around him when he wouldn't budge, heading to the main door. The moment her hand touched the handle, relief cascaded through her. She wanted to be anywhere else than here. Her worst-case scenario had come to fruition. She'd have to awkwardly face mystery man every day of her life.

****

Shadow knew his neighbor had been tailing him from the second he left his house. In fact, he knew everything about the curvy little number. Killer of Kings didn't hire fucking amateurs. He knew the asshole three blocks down smoked a cigarette on his front porch every night after sunset, the woman across the street was having an affair on her husband, and Riley Church had been on the streets since she was twelve years old.

What he didn't understand was why she wanted to follow him. He'd worked hard to create a veneer that masked his lifestyle, every detail to keep nosy neighbors at bay. No matter how hard he tried, it seemed a normal life wasn't in the cards for him.

When he'd made his appearance at the gym after watching from a distance, he didn't like the fear he saw in Riley's eyes. Shadow had wanted to teach her a lesson for her own damn good, choosing not to intervene right away. When he heard them taunting her, he wasn't expecting the rush of possessiveness that heated his blood. It took all his resolve not to pull out his Glock and start taking out the pricks one by one. But they were just mixed up young men, and they respected Shadow. Or maybe it was just fear.

He didn't have time to babysit a girl determined to get herself killed. And he sure as hell didn't need her digging around his private life. He'd lived in his house on the same street for almost ten years without issue. He refused to move. Boss had mentioned on numerous occasions that the best place for a hitman was a secure condo downtown or a stand-alone off the grid. Shadow knew he was playing house, trying to create the life he'd craved since childhood. It was all a fucking illusion, but it was a part of his humanity he refused to give up.

So his brave little neighbor needed to learn her place. The rest of the neighborhood kept their distance, and she needed to do the same. He had her on security camera at least a dozen times trying to snoop in his windows or peek over the backyard fence. Shadow hadn't thought much of her meddling until today. He hoped this scare had put some sense into her.

After finishing up his usual Thursday session at the gym, he headed home. He'd pushed himself harder than ever, and he knew Riley was to blame. He couldn't get her off his fucking mind. She only came up to his chest, and her curves were even thicker up close and personal. He ground his teeth together, trying not to think about digging his fingers into her rounded hips as he fucked her from behind. She was way too young for him, and he wasn't in the market for a woman anyway. His solitary life suited him.

It was nearly eleven, only the streetlights and faint glow of the moon illuminating his street. He pushed his entry fob and the garage door opened as he approached his house. His cellphone vibrated moments after entering the garage and cutting the engine.

"Yeah."

"I've left you alone for a while, but I have a job for you," said Boss.

It had been well over a month since Shadow had heard from Killer of Kings. The clean-up after they took down part of the Dead Angels MC was a fucking headache. He'd appreciated the time off, but he was ready to get back to work. His trigger finger was itching, and he needed an outlet stronger than the gym for the darkness growing inside him.

"You want to text me the details?"

"This job will require a bit of recon. I want to be sure we're getting the right man. He's used body doubles in the past. Can you handle that?" asked Boss.

In all the years Shadow had worked for Killer of Kings, he'd fucked up *one* time, giving Boss some bad intel. It wasn't like him, and sure as hell wouldn't let it happen again. Boss would probably hold that mistake over his head for years.

"Yeah, I can handle that."

"Good. Then I'll text you the details," said Boss before hanging up.

As much as he would love to direct his anger at Boss, he couldn't. Shadow had been a foster care runaway since before he could remember. He'd been a skinny, broken teen living on the streets, fighting to survive, when his guardian angel found him at seventeen. The older man had taken him in, showed him the first kindness he'd ever known, and taught him how to fight. He owed Mr. Karpenko everything.

After his tours of duty, his mentor had introduced him to Boss, and the world of Killer of Kings was opened up to him. Everyone working for Boss had to be fearless, ready to go to hell and back for a contract. Shadow wasn't afraid to live and die by the sword. His fear of death ran deeper, starting with his earliest blurred memories of his mother dying slowly from lung cancer. Mr. Karpenko had been one of Boss's many informants, and he respected the owner of Killer of Kings—that fact spoke volumes.

Shadow pushed his thoughts away and got out of his car. Just before he hit the panel inside the garage to close the door, he saw a shadow watching him. He immediately reached behind him, getting a good grip on his gun, keeping his hand at the ready.

"Who's there?"

"Sorry, it's your neighbor. I wanted to apologize for earlier."

He adjusted his stance, leaving the gun in his waistband. "For what?"

"You were right. I was following you. It was stupid, I know, but my curiosity got the better of me," she said.

Shadow narrowed his eyes, staring at Riley Church under the glow of the streetlights outside. She didn't know who she was fucking with. He'd lost count of his contracted kills. "Curiosity killed the cat, no?"

He refused to turn on the lights in the garage. Darkness had always been a friend in his line of work, and he didn't want to face her right now. Or ever.

"That was a really bad part of the city," she said, ignoring his comment.

"And?"

"Why were you there?"

This time he chuckled; he couldn't help himself. This chick wasn't his girlfriend or wife. Their only connection was the proximity of their houses. She either had balls of steel or a death wish. "You just apologized for following me, and now you're giving me an interrogation? Good luck with that, sweetheart."

"Right. Not my business," she said. "Thank you for saving me from those jerks."

Shadow needed to put an end to this before it got out of hand. He didn't need a friend, a woman, or a private eye invading his life. The only way to ensure she kept her distance was to put a little fear in her, because obviously the scare at the gym wasn't enough to set her straight.

He slapped his palm on the wall panel near her head, making her yelp. The double garage door began to lower. "Those gangbangers weren't your real problem," he said, slow and steady. "You should be worried about being alone with *me*."

Chapter Two

"You should be worried about being alone with me."

Riley nibbled her lip as she thought about her neighbor's last words before the garage door closed between them. That was a threat, wasn't it? What other way could it be taken? Sitting along at home, she'd locked all of the windows, doors, and was sitting at her dining room table, with the garlicy pasta she'd just cooked. His words went through her head, over and over again.

That place had been scary. It was a gym, but those men were going to hurt her. She'd seen the glint in their eyes, and she'd never been so terrified. Over the course of her life, she'd gotten into some difficult situations—men wanting a little more than she could give. It was all part of the course of living on the streets.

Sometimes she'd get caught and thrown back into the foster system. No one gave a shit about her, but she was street smart. Riley knew how to take care of herself. When a little randy daddy thought he could try it out on her, she'd held a knife to his dick, ready to take it off.

What she found most ironic about her times on the streets, was the fact the street people were the nicest people she'd been around. Maybe it was because she was a kid, or that she was in the same boat as them so to speak.

It was the other kind of people she had to watch out for—the predators, the ones that trolled the streets looking for easy targets. Riley had seen evil firsthand. She'd looked it in the eye, and stared death straight on.

When she'd been sixteen, a pimp had tried to get her to work for him. First, he'd tried to be nice, offering her food, drinks, and stuff like that, but she wasn't a vulnerable teen fresh on the street. She'd recognized the routine, and had been warned about it by a couple of the whores she knew. They'd told her not to accept anything unless it was at one of the shelters. She had to treat everyone as if they were the enemy, always expecting the worst. It was a depressing way to live.

Riley pulled herself out of her memories as she really didn't like delving into her past. She'd reinvented herself, working hard to get where she was with no help from anyone. She finished her pasta, washed her dish, and then made her way to her room. Her bedroom was in the back of the house, overlooking the garden, and she paused as she saw her mystery neighbor outside.

There was something very different about him. He didn't match the house, the street, the suburb. This neighborhood was all about falsehood. They would speak nicely to your face, and stab you in the back. Riley couldn't stand fake people.

Some of the guys were cheating on their wives with a few of the neighbors. She'd seen it all. She didn't fit in, would never be part of their little crowd, and something told her, neither did her neighbor. He was like her in a way.

Riley had looked death in the face, had seen pure evil up close, but there was something else about her neighbor. She didn't know what it was, but she couldn't stop obsessing over him. He made her curious, and for her, that in itself was a very dangerous thing.

What secrets was her neighbor hiding?

She didn't for a second believe that he was just some ordinary 9 to 5. Dangerous men like the ones at the gym didn't back away because of one look from a guy.

He'd given that away about himself, and it had only added to his intrigue.

The following day, as she was putting the

finishing touches on the birthday cake that was due to be picked up by three, she still hadn't fathomed what the deal was with him. She didn't have the time to be staring into space, wondering about one guy, and yet that was exactly what she was doing.

Come on, Riley, get a damn grip.

Once the cake was packaged and in the cooler to make sure the buttercream frosting didn't melt, she served out a couple of cookies, and made up some sandwiches for her regular customers. And then froze. Her neighbor was right outside of her shop, and he was talking with another man. She didn't recognize the guy, but the frown on her neighbor's face gave him an even more menacing look. He shook his head and told the guy that he shouldn't be there.

Had she seen right? Had he call the guy "boss"?

Was this one of those BDSM things?

Had she misread her mystery man entirely?

This was going to drive her crazy for, like, ever. She hated having one of these curious minds that demanded to know answers. Unless she was sure the answers were on the opposite side of the page, she never did a crossword puzzle. She liked answers to all of her questions, and if she didn't get them, it tended to ruin her entire day. She was that weird.

Suddenly, hot neighbor looked up, and saw her staring. This time, though, she raised a brow.

She watched as he said goodbye to the guy, and then moved toward her shop. Once he walked in the door, the delicious scent of his musky cologne wafted around her.

"Are you following me again?" he asked.

"I work here." She stared at him. "Why are you following *me*?"

"I'm not. That's your deal, remember?"

She smiled. Was he flirting with her? "I didn't leave my shop. I'm right here, and I've got nothing to hide."

"You're saying that I do?"

This was strange. "Of course not. Can I get you anything?" she asked.

He glanced down at the small display case she'd filled that morning with buns, cakes, and cookies, tapping his fingers on the glass. "You like to bake?" he asked.

Was he trying to make small talk? She had no clue. Everything about him was an enigma.

"Yeah, I do." After all she'd been through, she found baking relaxed her, and it gave her a purpose. There was something about creating a cake from scratch and turning it into something beautiful, that was what she loved more than anything else. It was her dream that her bakery be a little bigger, but right now she'd take whatever she could get. "What about you? What do you do?" she asked. If he asked her a question, she should be allowed the same rights.

"I handle several investments. I work from home."

His answer was vague, but she was shocked he gave her an answer at all. She glanced out of the window, and just couldn't help herself. "Are you gay?" She felt her cheeks heat since he looked a little taken aback. "It's not a problem or anything. I just … you were very close to that guy out there, and you were calling him boss. That's fine." She couldn't help but remember how scared those men were of him. *Stop rambling!*

"How did you know his name was Boss?" he asked, tilting his head to the side.

She had this uncanny way of reading lips. It had aided her when she was a street kid. "I saw you say his name. It's not that hard."

He did that frowning thing. "You can tell conversations from reading someone's lips?"

Okay, he was starting to take a really big interest in that, and she no longer felt comfortable with this. "I better get to work. Do you want anything?"

"Yeah," he said, rounding the counter into her private space.

"Hey, this is my bakery, and right now you're stepping over personal boundaries."

He grabbed her arm, and took her toward the window. She liked how firm his grip was on her arm. She didn't reach for her knife, but she was tempted for a second.

"What are they saying?" he asked, pointing to a man and woman.

She'd gotten his interest, which now she was wishing she really hadn't. Blowing out a breath, she decided to play along. What was wrong with a bit of fun? She'd done this so often to keep herself amused over the years.

"You've got to stop texting me. My wife is getting suspicious," she said. "I can only see if they don't move. The woman I can't see. She's got her back to us."

"What about that couple there?" He pointed people sitting on an indoor bench in one of the other stores. They were quite far, and she shook her head.

"I can read lips. I don't have bionic eyes." She pulled out of his hold. "What were you doing at that gym?"

"Working out."

"They were afraid of you. Why?" She folded her arms, challenging him.

Never in all of her life had she ever gone this personal before, or this invasive. From the moment she had started, she knew she had to stop. The words were just tumbling out as if they had a mind of their own.

He didn't say a word.

"What's your name?" she asked. "That's a fair question. You grabbed me, manhandled me right to first base. I think I have a right to know your name."

He smirked. "I'll tell you my name when you earn it." He left her shop after a wink, and a rush of frustration took her by surprise. Putting her hands back on her hips, she walked behind the counter. She would find out everything about him.

Even with his threat ringing in her head, she didn't care. She wanted to know who her neighbor was. Her bullshit sense was tingling, and that guy was filled with a whole lot of it.

****

Shadow watched from a dark corner as Riley closed up her shop. She didn't even realize that he'd been keeping tabs on her all day. He'd underestimated her, that was for sure. When she had said Boss's name, he'd nearly given himself away. Of course, he almost died of laughter when she asked if he was gay. He had nothing against being gay, he just most definitely wasn't. Women were his thing, but he loved it when they didn't have hearts and flowers in their eyes. He wasn't a good man.

His life at Killer of Kings had made it so. Being a killer came naturally to him. What he wanted was to fit in. He'd been to Viper's, Killian's, and Bain's special lockup homes. They were like fortresses, and were constantly guarded.

He liked the idea of being an ordinary guy, something that had eluded him his entire life. What he hadn't expected was having a very nosy neighbor, which was exactly what Riley was.

She was intrusive, but he believed her ability to read lips was a unique gift that he could use to his advantage. He'd have to be careful around her. Boss hadn't wanted to text him any vital information in case it got hacked, and seeing as Shadow had a photographic memory, all he needed was to be told or to look at something, and he'd remember. That was one of his skills.

One look at a map, and he'd remember it for the rest of his life. The skill had served him well in the military and during his life as a hitman.

With his latest mission from Boss, the man had no name as he was constantly changing faces. The asshole was wanted in several countries for just about every crime imaginable. Boss had contracts from numerous sources, so it would be a big pay day once this guy was in the ground.

It wasn't always about money for Boss. In his spare time, he liked to help certain causes. Shadow knew firsthand that Boss's heart wasn't all black, and one of his pet peeves was the human trafficking of women and children. About five years ago, Shadow had been hunting a man who'd stolen a wealthy man's kid. He paid top dollar for his safe return. They'd discovered a black market specializing in the smuggling of women and kids. It had sickened Shadow, but Boss, he made sure every man involved lived to regret it. He hunted them down, and declared war on anyone who had anything to do with it. Shadow had witnessed Boss torture a woman who had beaten kids into submission so they could be sold. There was a lot of sick shit in the world.

With Riley's back to him, Shadow moved in until he was standing directly behind her. He kept to the shadows because he could blend in. No one would ever hear him.

"You're closing up late," he said.

She gasped and spun around. Riley reached in her

purse, pulling out a blade and holding it in front of her.

When recognition softened her features, she lowered her arm. "I don't like to be sneaked up on," she said. "What do you want?"

"You didn't use that knife last night." He noticed she didn't shake. What had happened to her that made her so confident in holding a knife?

"I didn't think I'd need it. You told me you were the real threat, anyway. I live next door to you. If you don't give me your name, I'm going to start calling you Ghost."

Shadow smirked. He had never met a woman like her. She was a fighter through and through. "I need a ride home," he lied.

She put the blade away, and took a step back. "Okay. Jump in."

Riley was a mystery that was for damn sure. Climbing into the passenger seat of the car, he watched her drive. She didn't try to make small talk, and for several minutes silence filled the car—besides her noisy muffler.

"My name's Shadow," he said, giving her the truth.

Riley snorted. "Really? That didn't take long for me to earn that pesky trust. What did I do?"

"You caught me by surprise with the knife."

"You can't be too safe."

"It's not exactly a bad neighborhood," he said.

"That's why I like it—even if I don't fit in. And I've lived beside you for a little while now, and if you've been trying to blend in, you've failed. You stick out as much as I do. I don't mind either. It's good to be a little different. At least I keep trying to convince myself it's good." She tucked some hair behind her ear, and it made him want to reach out, to wrap a curl around his finger.

He didn't.

"How do we stick out?"

"We don't feel the need to join in. We're not fakes. We don't need to pretend to be something we're not. I'm used to being on my own. I cleaned tables in a strip club when I was fourteen." She laughed as she told him.

"How?" he asked.

"I convinced the guy that I was better and cheaper, proved it, too. Got paid a hundred bucks a week to clean up beer. It was easy money, and I didn't have to turn tricks to get it." She parked in her driveway, and turned toward him. "Half of the people in this neighborhood don't get that. They're ignorant of what happens in the real world." She climbed out of the car, and he did the same.

"You're not going to be following me tonight?" he asked. Not that he had any intention of going anywhere. His only date was with his computer to memorize everything he could about his latest mission. It wasn't going to be easy, and he had a feeling this one was going to take more time than a simple find and eliminate.

"Nope. Tonight, I'm really tired. I want some food and relaxation. Besides, I got to know your name. Have a nice night, *Shadow*." She waved her hand, and left him alone.

Shadow didn't linger, even though he found her voice soothing. Instead, he made his way inside his home, and found Boss already waiting for him.

"You took your time getting home," Boss said. He was sitting in the corner, reading a magazine.

"I got waylaid."

Boss nodded. "She going to be a problem?" He pointed behind him, clearly at Riley's home.

"No. She's not." Talking with her had been the

SAM CRESCENT & STACEY ESPINO

most fun he'd experienced in a long time. She was cute,
different. He didn't want Boss to kill her. "That file you
got on her didn't have everything that was important.
You need to tell Maurice to do better."

"He got everything that was legal."

"What do you mean everything that was legal?"
Shadow asked. He cared a little too much about this
woman. What he needed to do was get his damn head
back in the game and fast.

"Everyone has two different lives. There's only so
much you can find out online. Medical records, stuff like
that. I give out the information that people ask for, and let
them know that they should make their own judgments,
and that includes you as well. The file only has half the
truth about her. You've got to dig deeper to find the real
shit."

Shadow nodded. "I'll keep that in mind." She'd
gone from being a boring bakery owner with a rough
past, to something a hell of a lot more interesting.

The fact she had the nerve to pull a blade on him
made getting to know her worth his time. Of course, he'd
never been in danger. But it was cute that she'd tried to
threaten him. He loved this neighborhood, even all the
fake assholes that lived around him. In between his work,
he could see himself enjoying the distraction of
unraveling Riley.

"Tell me again why you couldn't give me this file
in an email?" Shadow asked, pointing at the folder on
Boss's lap.

"This guy has been in hiding for years. No one
has ever gotten a shot at him. The thing is, he likes to
take on new identities, new faces, which is what makes it
harder for him to be caught. He's got a few body doubles
on top of that. From what I've been told, he knows when
someone is onto him, and it makes him scarper. I don't

want to risk that. Handle this one with extreme care. No mistakes, no big clean-ups. What I need from you is to be one hundred percent certain you know it's the right guy. I don't care how long it takes, but do it as if it was a hobby. Be certain, be thorough."

"I get it. Take my time, no mess, no clean-ups. I get it, Boss."

"Good." Boss got up, and left without another word.

Shadow stared down at the file. This was his life. He was the one that kept to the shadows and found people who didn't want to be found. Killian could handle the job, but he always came with a lot of noise. Shadow kept quiet, and he knew Boss appreciated that.

He walked down into his basement after disarming the security measures. After flicking on the light, he turned on all the computer screens, and watched Riley sitting at her table.

While she'd been at work that morning, he'd gone in and wired her entire house. She couldn't make a move without him knowing about it, and he didn't feel any remorse about that either.

Chapter Three

"I'm not paid enough for this shit," Riley muttered under her breath. The woman from down the street didn't have time to pick up her cake and pastry order for her party, so she'd called Riley and begged her to drop everything off at her house. Riley was supposed to be coming to the anniversary party as a guest, but she had no plans of actually showing up.

Now she had to juggle the huge cake box and several smaller boxes as she tried to fit them in her cramped Toyota Corolla. She didn't do deliveries because her car barely made it to work and back. The parking lot was usually close to empty when she left every night, but today it was bustling as the new tenant was busy setting up the bar for its grand opening tomorrow.

Once finally settled in the driver's seat, she carefully drove out of the plaza, heading to her client's house. She was terrified the cake would shift in the box or get damaged before she arrived. It was a lot of pressure baking for a bunch of neighbors that already saw her as the black sheep of the suburb.

The street was lined with parked cars for the party so she just settled in her own driveway, making her trek with all the cake boxes precarious at best. By the time she reached the house, she was out of breath. Music flooded out onto the sidewalk. Luckily there were some smokers on the front porch, so they opened the door for her. She found the nearest counter and set down her load, her arms grateful for the break.

"Oh, Carol, thank you," said Amanda, appearing through the throngs of guests.

"It's Riley," she corrected.

"Right…" Amanda put her hands on her hips and gave her a less than discreet once over. Everyone wore their evening best, and Riley had her flour-stained scrubs on. She looked and felt completely out of place, and she hated that all-too-familiar feeling of being belittled. Her entire life had been a struggle. As an adult she'd put up barriers, convincing herself she didn't give a shit about anyone else's opinion. Reality wasn't always so simple.

"Your order is all there. It should be refrigerated."

"Will your husband be joining you?" asked Amanda. Karen came up behind her friend, adjusting a sheer sash over her shoulder. Surely they knew Riley was alone and single. Of course they did. It was like high school all over again.

"Erm, no, it's just me."

She wanted to run, to be in the sanctuary of her own home. This wasn't her crowd, not that she'd ever been a people person.

When a warm hand landed on her hip from behind, she jerked. Nobody was allowed to touch her without permission. She turned around, ready to tell the asshole to keep his hands to himself.

It was him.

Mystery neighbor.

Shadow.

"Are you ready to go?" he asked.

After remembering how to speak, she answered. "Yeah, I'm ready."

Riley loved the look of shock on the other women's faces. They appeared as dumb-founded as she felt. Still, she wasn't going to waste this chance to get the hell out of Dodge.

"Keep it down," Shadow said to Amanda. "Some of us have to work in the morning." He led Riley to the front door with a hand to the small of her back. She didn't object, not just because she was thankful to be leaving, but she liked his touch. More than she should.

Once they were outside on the sidewalk, she stopped and faced him, pressing a hand to his chest to keep him in place. "What was that?"

"What do you mean?" He wore all black, smart casual pants and open collared shirt. He cleaned up nice, but she always thought he was gorgeous in that brooding sort of way.

"Really? I mean, where are you supposed to be taking me?"

"You're smarter than that, Riley." The man had no expression, a blank slate with those same evil eyes. The evening dusk gave him a menacing aura. Her instincts told her she should be afraid, but she wasn't.

She exhaled, running a hand through her hair. "I was saving you. You told me you couldn't stand fake people."

"Why were *you* there? Trying to get lucky?" Riley couldn't help herself. Half the time when she should keep her mouth shut, it kept on running.

He frowned. "I'm not interested in spoiled bitches." Shadow began walking toward their end of the street.

Riley bit her bottom lip, following along with him. She'd assumed even her reclusive neighbor would fall for the Barbie doll looks of Amanda and her friends. "Well, thanks for that. You don't have to leave because of me," she said.

"I wasn't there to socialize, just help you out. According to your rules, that should earn me a question."

She smiled. "Sure, ask away."

The street lights flicked on, the music from the party fading as they neared their homes. "You were in foster care since you were twelve. What happened before that?"

"I never told you that." Her nerves flared up. How

could he know that about her?

"If you were busting tables at fourteen to avoid turning tricks, I guarantee you were a foster kid," he said. "What happened before that?"

This guy might be nosier than she was. Riley owed him an answer, but his question was way more invasive than asking for a simple name. She didn't like to venture that far into her memories. They were vile, and she wished she could erase them from her head completely.

"Why do you care?"

"I have an inquiring mind. Considering you like to spy on me, I want to know what I'm dealing with."

She frowned, grating her teeth. Her first reaction was to tell him to "fuck off". She was good at that, putting up walls and keeping people at bay. But he was right. Riley had been snooping on him because her curious mind drove her crazy if she ignored it. She still refused to admit the truth.

They stopped in front of their driveways. She turned to face him, her hands defensively on her hips. "My childhood isn't anyone's business but mine. Besides, it has nothing to do with who I am today."

"I beg to differ."

"Then your childhood must have been really fucked up," she said. Riley immediately regretted her words. She sounded like a bitch, but she was used to protecting herself with words when she felt threatened.

"It was."

Then he walked up the path to his front door without another word. Riley felt like a royal ass. The guy had saved her from the party, walked her home, and asked a question. What was wrong with her?

Part of her wanted to chase after him and apologize. Again. She had no clue what this guy's history was, and more than anyone, she knew what it was like to have a miserable childhood.

She watched him enter his house before going home. How had he known she needed saving from the party? Why did he care? A tiny piece of her heart hoped and wondered if he liked her. Relationships didn't exactly work out for her—ever. She liked sex, liked men, but the long-term thing always fell flat. Riley was convinced she attracted assholes, keeping her dream of a normal happily ever after out of reach. Maybe staying away from Shadow was in her best interest.

For the next week, she barely saw her neighbor. She'd seen him leave the house once, and he put out his trash as usual. He ignored her as he had since she moved in, but it just felt awkward now.

After closing up late the next Friday night, the parking lot was already full, a mix of cars and motorcycles. The new bar in the plaza was attracting an unsavory crowd. A few of the units had already complained, and they'd only been open for a week. Riley didn't really care since she was usually closed for the day before they started getting rowdy.

She'd just put her keys in her car lock when Janet rushed her from behind. "Riley!"

"Don't sneak up on someone like that," she said, clutching her chest.

"I can't work like this anymore," Janet said. "I can't even get to my car."

"Why not?"

"It's over there. I'm scared to go near those creeps." Janet held her suit jacket shut tight as she glanced over the top of the car to the other end of the lot.

"Do you want me to walk you to your car?" Riley asked.

Janet exhaled. "Would you?"

Riley nodded, putting her keys back in her purse. "No problem." After the life she'd lived, rough guys and drunks didn't scare her. "You should park in front of your office next time."

"I know. I will," said Janet. "I don't usually leave this late, but I had a lot of paperwork to finish."

They walked across the lot together. The loud laughter and cursing mingled with the music from the bar. The door was propped open, and a group of men were outside. Riley smelled pot, and it churned her stomach. She'd moved out to the suburbs to get away from this type of shit.

Once they came into view, the old guys stared whistling and firing off the crude catcalls.

"Just ignore them. They're like feral dogs, don't look them in the eye," said Riley. She waited for her friend to get safely in her car, and then she stood back as she backed out of her parking space. Janet gave her a little wave before she disappeared from view.

"Come on over here, doll," a gruff voice called out. "I have a surprise for you."

Riley cringed as she walked away, putting up her middle finger without a backward glance. Drunks disgusted her, especially drunks that hit on her at eight o'clock when she just wanted to get home from work.

"Fat bitch!"

She rolled her eyes and got into her car. If there was one thing she was used to, it was insults. Riley didn't allow other people's opinions to affect her. Or at least she tried. It was another part of the wall she built around herself to keep from getting hurt. She loved her body and took care of herself. There were so many times she could have said yes to drugs and turning tricks, but she respected herself too much for that. It had been a constant fight for her, and it was one she was determined to win.

Riley pulled into her driveway, her mood spoiled despite her attempts to push the rude comments away. Did Shadow think she was too fat? *Stop torturing yourself, Riley!* Tonight, she'd take a nice long bath after dinner to unwind. She'd let the rest of the world slip away and get lost in a good book or just close her eyes and let her mind wander as she soaked in the bubbles. It sounded like a good plan to her.

By the time she went to bed that night, she expected a solid night's sleep—not to be woken by her phone sounding off at 2:40 AM. When she sat up to check who was calling, it was the alarm at her bakery. She frowned. There was nothing of real value to steal, except day old baked goods that she'd throw out in the morning. Then she remembered the expensive mixers and supplies she kept in the back and her heart started racing.

She struggled to get dressed while fighting off her grogginess. Riley prayed it was a false alarm.

****

Shadow had wanted to find out more about Riley Church. He'd been obsessing over her since that night with the knife. The thought of a problem living next door, a woman who could unravel his secrets, didn't sit well with him, so he needed information. Since she refused to give him anything, he got what he could from a bit of deeper digging by Maurice—more but not all. The real story needed to come from Riley.

Since his own contract was still in the recon stage, he'd had plenty of time to watch Riley on the large screens in his basement. He had her routine memorized. It had very little deviation, except tonight when she came home two hours later than normal.

She paced the hallway, her little hands in tight fists. Something had happened to upset her, and he reminded himself he needed to wire her bakery, too.

When she began stripping off her clothes in the bedroom, he flicked off the screen. He didn't need to see more. Riley already had him facing every day with blue balls. He'd always been proficient at keeping his emotions and desires in check. There wasn't a fucking woman in the world who could get into his head or tempt him into her bed—until now. The little troublemaker with the wicked curves had gotten under his skin, and he wasn't sure how to deal with it.

Love at first sight was a joke, something invented for cheap chick flicks. It certainly didn't pertain to a man who'd devoted himself to killing for a living, a man who vowed never to let his emotions come first. Shadow didn't need or want a family. Then why couldn't he put Riley out of his head? Why was he ready to kill for her?

That night, the motion sensors he had set up at Riley's house went off, waking him up. He barely had time to see her speed out of her driveway in the dead of night. *Fuck!*

Where would she be going at this hour? Once again, he shouldn't care. She was crazy, and a huge complication to his chosen lifestyle. But instead of heading back to bed like he wanted to, he was busy checking the clips on his Glocks. He had a glass of orange juice as he pinpointed the GPS location of her car on his cellphone. She was heading back to her bakery.

He set the glass in the sink, grabbed his jacket, and headed out.

The plaza was usually empty at this hour. He'd met with Boss and other contacts in the lot at night countless times, and it had never looked like this. The bar on the corner was no sports grill like advertised. It was a drinking hole for bikers and lowlifes. They'd taken over half the parking lot. Shadow stopped on the periphery and watched Riley walking around inside her bakery. He decided to move in closer and investigate.

Shadow turned off his ignition and walked across the lot to the bakery. As he got closer, the light inside contrasted with the darkness outside, allowing him to see her tears. The front window was smashed in. He opened the front door and walked in, making Riley flinch until she saw it was him. Broken glass crunched beneath his boots.

She used the back of her sleeve to remove any evidence of tears. "What are you doing here?"

"I saw you rush off. I was concerned."

"So you followed me?"

He ignored her, assessing the damage as he strode around. "I'm guessing it was just one of those drunks getting rowdy," he said.

"No, this was intentional." Riley handed him a brick with a note attached to it. He removed the rubber band and read it: *Stay out of our plaza FAT BITCH!*

She shrugged. "Whatever, right? I should have seen this coming. I mean, my own bakery … dreams don't come true for girls like me." Riley tried to replicate disinterest, but she wasn't fooling him.

"Have you called the police?" he asked.

"Not yet."

"Good."

He left the bakery, heading toward the bar. Riley rushed behind him.

"Wait, where are you going?"

"Whoever did this to you has to pay," he said.

"Stop! I have insurance. Don't be stupid, Shadow." She tugged on the arm of his jacket, so he stopped.

"You're not the type to let assholes walk all over you. If this bakery is your dream, then you have to fight for it."

"It's not so simple," she said.

"Yeah, well, it is for me."

He knew where Riley was coming from. Shadow had worked his way up from nothing. His mother had died of cancer when he was a boy, and then it was a mix of foster care and the streets after that. His life had been no picnic, but even though he had everything now, and more money than he could ever spend, he didn't have what he really wanted.

Riley's pleas turned to whispers as they approached the bar.

"Shadow, don't…"

"Stay here," he said. "I'll have a word with the owner. I'm sure it can be handled diplomatically."

"Are you kidding me?"

He scanned the crowd of men outside the bar, many older than he was, a few younger. He counted eight. There were a couple wearing cuts, which made things more complicated. Which one had thrown the brick, he wondered. He planned to find out.

"Who's the owner of this bar?" he asked.

"Fuck off," said one of the men, a cigarette hanging from his lips.

"He's with *her*," said another.

Shadow cleared his throat. He didn't have a short temper like some of his colleagues. Rushing in with guns blazing wasn't his style. Besides, this place was too close to home, a place he liked to keep separate from his other persona.

"I'll find him myself," said Shadow, pushing through the group of unruly men. When one of them gave him a firm shove, a switch flicked inside of him. Shadow hated bullies. He turned to the side and punched the man square in the face, sending him toppling down.

Riley screamed.

He'd started something now, something he planned to finish. Even though there were a lot of them, he wanted to handle it as quietly as possible. He'd already decided the bar had to go. That was on his to-do list for later. Shadow had made the decision the second he knew why there were tears in Riley's eyes.

"Where's the owner of the fucking bar?" he repeated, his voice carrying a distinct threat.

"You have a death wish?" The men began surrounding him. He could smell the smoke and cheap booze on their breath behind him.

"Someone put a brick through the bakery window. I want to know who it was," he said.

"And if we don't say anything?"

Shadow squatted down and pulled out his butterfly knife from the side of his boot. He began to play with it, the blade and handles spinning and flying round his fingers and wrist with expert accuracy. He'd perfected his skills with a blade over the years, almost as flawless as his expertise behind a sniper rifle. The crowd stood transfixed until the first fool made a move for his knife. Shadow stabbed him in the arm as a warning. This entire show was his attempt to keep thing as civil as possible, with the least collateral damage.

His patience was endless. Or so it seemed.

"Leave while you can, or next time it'll be more than your girl's window you have to worry about."

In a flash, Shadow turned and had his blade pressed against the man's carotid artery. "What the fuck did you just say?" His instinct to protect Riley was off the fucking chart. The thought of one of these bastards putting their filthy hands on her, made him all too eager to take every one of them out. Fuck the consequences. He didn't even recognize himself.

"N-nothing."

"Any of you so much as breathes on her, I'll kill you."

"You taking a knife to a gunfight, junior?" He felt the muzzle of a gun at the back of his head. Why couldn't they leave well enough alone?

"Shadow!" Riley called out.

He smirked. It would have been fun to have Killian by his side about now. It would be a good time regardless. Shadow squatted, turned and brought his knife up into the man's throat, blood spraying out in every direction. When the man's gun dropped, Shadow kicked it away.

Then he saw the asshole with the beard holding Riley in front of him, his arm across her neck. "I'll kill her," he shouted. "Drop your knife."

Shadow stood up straight, slowly, methodically.

He tossed his knife on the pavement and began walking forward.

When the old bastard thought he'd won, Shadow pulled his Glock from his shoulder holster, aimed, and nailed him right between the eyes. Riley screamed, backing away from the body as it dropped in a heap. It only took seconds for him to curse his decision. Riley had just gone from neighbor to witness, and Boss wouldn't like it.

What was he thinking? He could have handled this without a body count. Fuck, he shouldn't even be here. Riley made him act completely out of character.

"Come here," he said, holding out his hand.

Riley ran over to him, her face blanched. She held his hand, and he made his way inside the bar. The music still played, most of the patrons taking cover after witnessing the gun show outside. Once in the middle of the bar, he called out, "Who owns this place?"

A couple people pointed out one man sitting at the

end of the bar. Shadow approached him.

"One of your customers broke a window at the bakery. You aware of that shit?"

The man shook his head.

"You'll be paying for the damage?"

He nodded.

"If it happens again, I mean *anything*, I'll come after you, your family, and your pocketbook. Understand?"

When he nodded again, Shadow repeated himself more loudly. "Do you *understand*?"

"Yes."

Shadow wanted to do a hell of a lot more, but he restrained his urge to bring a firestorm of hurt on the asshole.

As they walked out of the bar, heading back to the bakery, Riley hadn't said a word. She was tough, but not many were used to Shadow's world of blood and carnage. Maybe a bit of humor would help. "If you went through insurance, your rates would go up," he said. "It's better this way."

Chapter Four

Riley couldn't believe that she'd just witnessed a bloodbath, and she wasn't running away screaming. She cleaned up debris on her bakery floor as Shadow pinned up some boards to cover her smashed window.

He hadn't said a word, and neither had she.

They worked in silence.

What was even scarier than this mess? What had gone down at the bar wasn't the worst thing she'd ever seen. Being on the streets, she'd seen men completely torture others and then leave them for the rats. One thing she'd learned, never ask too many questions. And no one really wanted to know the answers.

"You're full of surprises," Shadow said.

"Huh?"

"Usually I'm the one hoping someone else will shut the fuck up, but right now I'm hoping you'll talk." He stared at her with his arms folded. Shadow wore dark gray joggers and a white wife-beater under his jacket. His body was rock hard, and she had to remember not to stare too long. It was nearly time for her to get things ready for work. Her day started before dawn. The life of a baker never stopped. "Talk, Riley."

"What do you want me to say?"

"You saw me shoot a man, and even though there was a scream from you, you're not telling the police?"

She nibbled her lip. "Police are no good. They tend to cause more trouble than they fix. I don't trust them."

Shadow had actually helped her. Why would she report him for protecting her?

The insurance company would completely cripple her if she was to make a claim. They already demanded enough as it was. Half of her problem was the outrageous rent on her unit. She couldn't catch a break.

"That's a big … judgment you have."

"Believe it or not, I'd rather trust you than a cop." She poured the broken shards into the trash, and then stood, holding onto her shoulders. She really just wanted to cry. This was not how she wanted to start her day.

Maybe she really was fighting a losing battle to keep this dream alive, to make something of herself. Most of the kids she'd known growing up were addicts, dead, or in jail. She wanted so much more.

She released a breath.

"Again, you're not talking."

"I don't know what to say, Shadow." She dropped her hands, and looked around the small space. "I think it could be time to sell up. To face reality that some people get what they want, and others have no chance in hell of ever getting it."

"All you want is a bakery?"

"A successful one. I don't want millions or to go jet setting around. I just want a bakery that has people coming back for more. It's been my dream for as long as I can remember." She shrugged. What good were dreams when they were crumbling down around her?

"You don't strike me as a quitter."

She stared at him. He brought out so many of her feelings to the surface—the desire to be wanted, the need to put up more walls. "You shouldn't be thinking about me."

"Why not? I think about you. That's why I'm here."

Riley stopped. "Nobody's ever helped me before." She knew nothing about Shadow. Instead of worrying about the dead bodies at the other side of the plaza, he was looking at her in ways that made her heart race.

"I don't normally help women out of uncomfortable situations, but I've got some free time on my hands. Those guys could be trouble for you. I'm thinking of sticking around for a little while." He sat down on one of her chairs. "I like this place."

She wasn't really sure if she should take him seriously or not. Distrust came naturally to her. "I just watched you kill two guys. The way you fought... I've never seen anything like it."

"Yeah, spattered his useless brains all over the place. Probably the best thing I could have done," he said. Then he looked directly at her. "I didn't like his hands on you."

Putting a hand to her forehead, she closed her eyes, counting to ten. "You know this doesn't bode well for me. Are you like a hitman or something?"

"Or something." He winked at her.

"This is way too much for me, and way too early. I need coffee."

"I'll have a coffee. I'll have some cream and sugar, too."

He'd literally killed for her. The least she could do was get him a coffee. He also offered to be her personal bodyguard, and right now she didn't want to be alone. No one else in her life ever cared what happened to her or what someone did to her. This man, her neighbor, pretty much a stranger to her, had taken a life for her. In a weird way, she was kind of touched.

Shadow was really sexy to look at, so at least she won't mind the view. No, she shouldn't be thinking about how sexy he was, or the fact she liked looking at him, or that she thought it was sweet he killed someone. That was what made her weird.

Making them both some coffee, she also toasted up some bread, and found Shadow at the table clicking away on his cell phone. Putting a plateful of toast on the table, and his coffee in front of him, she took a seat. "You don't have to stick around, you know?"

"I've already organized a new sheet of glass. They should have it here within a couple hours." He grabbed his coffee. "I've got nothing else to do."

"A window company that comes that fast at this time of day?" she asked, intrigued by him. "And what kind of job do you have that means you don't have to go to work every single day?"

"The one that makes me the boss."

She stared at him recalling the conversation she witnessed the other week. "You're not the boss."

He tensed up. "How do you figure?"

"The way that guy talked to you. He's your boss. I could tell." She took a sip of her coffee.

"You're way too observant."

She looked up at him. "I've had to be."

"Yeah, why is that?"

Riley laughed. "You really want to know about my past, don't you?"

"You said someone like you doesn't get to have your dreams. Tell me about *you*, Riley."

She sighed. "That's just me having a pity party. Ignore me."

"Is that why you're alone?"

She frowned, wondering if she'd missed something. "I don't—"

"You've got no man in your life. There's no best friend. You're a loner, and you hate being around fake people. I saw the look on your face at the party. You didn't want to be there. You close up whenever anyone gets too close."

He'd nailed her spot on, and her barriers instantly went up. How could this stranger unravel her after a few words? "You know, I don't have to listen to any of this. Thank you so much for dealing with this stuff, but maybe you should go."

She took a slice of toast and her coffee, leaving him alone. Entering the kitchen, she tore into her toast, and began to preheat the oven.

"You also run away from everyone and everything."

"Screw you." She turned to face him. "You're not this squeaky-clean guy, just so you know. You're a mystery. You're as much of an outcast as I am."

"So, I'm not trying to be something I'm not."

"And I am?" She glared at him, feeling like a cornered dog.

"What do you call this?"

"This is my dream, asshole. Is this what you want? You want real? Fine. All my life I was the piece of shit that everyone wanted to be rid of. The kid no one wanted, not even my own parents. I've always been either too fat or too ugly. The foster system was no cake walk. It was worse than the streets. That's what I know. My bakery, it's mine. I can do one thing that's good, and I bake. I'm good at that. Actually, you know what, I'm fucking great. I've seen the looks on people's faces when they try something I've made, and it means everything to me."

"The suburban house?"

"It's a nice neighborhood. Why shouldn't I live here? The people might be fake, but this is the life I've always dreamed of." She was panting now, her anger at a fever pitch.

"Is that how you can read lips?" he asked. "The streets."

This made her frown. "What does it matter if I can read lips? Growing up, it saved me. I was able to know when shit was going to go bad."

Silence fell between them, and she kept on staring at him, waiting for him to say something else.

He held his hands up. "I'm sorry."

She took a cleansing breath. "Yeah. Me, too. I think the early morning murder and mayhem has messed with my head."

Shadow smirked. Why did he have to look so damn sexy when she tried to hate him? "I'm going to stick around to make sure they stay away from this place."

"If I die because you started something, I'm so going to come back as a ghost and haunt your ass."

"I look forward to the company."

He walked toward the front, looking out the good panes of glass.

"Maybe in death I'll finally figure out *your* secrets," she said.

Shadow turned back toward her. "Maybe one day I'll show you exactly what I am."

She didn't like that he made her crave to know more about him. He was just some guy, not important to her in the slightest, and yet, here she was, panting after him like a damn schoolgirl.

She had to be strong and focus on the day's baking, and ignore the sexy man and the last few hours.

Once she finished the toast and had her hair wrapped her up, she was ready to begin the day's baking. Riley was good at blocking out reality and carrying on in spite of it. Instead of worrying about bodies, police, money, and Shadow, she started baking some cupcakes. She was in a brownie cupcake mood. Every now and again she'd peek a look around the kitchen and find Shadow playing with his phone.

"Stop looking at him. Stop caring what he's

doing. You don't care that he's this super-hot guy that stuck up for you."

She made sure to whisper her little beratement so that he didn't hear her. He was the first guy in all of her life to actually give a shit and stick up for her. As much as she didn't want to care, it made her heart flutter, made her feel special.

Once the cupcakes were cooling, she made up the chocolate fudge frosting. Time went nowhere, and before long, she'd gotten everything baked, and her mind was still all over the place. The moment the counter was filled, and she felt like herself again, she nodded at Shadow to open the door. He did so without a second glance at her.

What did he think when he looked at her?

Why did she even care what he thought? It wasn't like they were ever going to get together. He could get anyone he wanted. And she couldn't stand him.

Total lie.

She didn't like how she couldn't get him off her mind. He managed to calm her temper, make her smile.

The window company came as promised, leaving her store better than when it started.

"I'll pay you back for that," she said. "It might take me a while."

Shadow shook his head. "I didn't ask for your money."

When some of her early clients came in, she was waiting for comments on the crime scene outside. She'd refused to look, wishing it had all been a bad dream. They said nothing.

Riled dared to peek out across the parking lot when she looked at the new window.

"How is that possible?" she whispered.

"What?"

"It's like nothing happened. Two men died over there. This isn't possible…"

"I took care of it."

Again with the riddles. Who the hell was Shadow?

There was a lull, so she decided to people watch. One woman read a list of instructions, and Riley smirked.

"What do you see?" Shadow asked. He'd got up and moved closer to her, and even though she wanted to ignore him, she didn't, and instead told him.

"The woman on the bench is reading a form on how to treat constipation." The woman's lips were moving, and she found it funny that no one else knew what the woman was doing.

"That's a pretty good gift."

"It's nothing." She looked toward another woman who was talking on her phone in the parking lot. "That woman there needs a doctor's appointment. She has itching down below, and thinks it's herpes."

"It must keep you entertained to know other people's secrets."

"It passes the time, and I don't know everyone's secrets."

****

Later that night Shadow was spending way too much time in his basement watching Riley. She was … unique, different, and he didn't know what to make of her. Today she'd been a mixture of fire and ice. Not once did she go to the police or put a call through. The window had been repaired, and he'd supervised the guys who did the job.

One of them had been trying to hit on Riley, to get her number and ask her out. There was no way in hell he was allowing that to happen, so he'd told them that she belonged to him. She was his woman.

Damn it.

This was not supposed to be complicated, and yet that was exactly what was happening. Shadow's life with Killer of Kings was extreme—murder and everything seedy in the world. Riley was right about him. He was living a lie, just like she was. Shadow lived in the suburb because he was essentially playing house. The feeling of normalcy gave him a high, even if counterfeit, because it had always been out of reach.

Running a finger along his lip, he watched as she leaned across her bed to grab the far book. It was one for frostings, and had so many notes scrawled over the pages. She had notes everywhere, which were all about baking.

All day he'd watched and listened as she worked. Her passion was her shop. It was her one place in the world that no one could take away from her.

The insurance company was a dodgy one. He didn't like it. The owner of the plaza was even worse, charging rents that were through the roof, and Riley didn't have any protection from any of that shit. He didn't like it when the big men took advantage of others. She just wanted to make a life for herself.

He got up from the basement, and grabbed a couple of beers from his fridge. Not caring that it was a little after eleven, he jumped the fence into her backyard, grabbed a stone, and threw it at her window.

Shadow was an expert marksman, and if he wanted to, he'd have totally smashed the glass. He wanted her attention, not to cause her more trouble.

Seconds passed, and when he threw a second stone, she finally came to the window.

"What the hell are you doing?" she asked, leaning outside. The negligee she wore was a cotton one with a cute little duck on the front. It was totally the opposite of what he expected her to wear, and yet it suited her.

"Want to share a beer?" he asked, holding up the bottles.

"Really?"

"Don't you want to know more about me?"

He wasn't about to tell her a damn thing. Still, he wanted a beer, and he liked her company. She wasn't like most women who demanded attention. Riley didn't ask him if she looked good, and didn't constantly check her appearance. What he really wanted was to take his dual lifestyle to the next level. He wanted to come home after a day of killing to the love of a good woman. But that wasn't possible.

Boss had already called him and torn him a new asshole, or tried to for causing a stir at the bar. He didn't give a shit about what Boss thought. All that mattered was the message that got across loud and clear—he had to leave Riley, and her bakery, alone. The cleanup crew had handled the aftermath in less than an hour. It was like the incident never happened, but Boss wouldn't forget so easily.

She opened the back door, and now she was wearing some kind of long cardigan that covered up way too much.

Taking a seat on one of her deck chairs, he waited for her to take the bottle from him.

"This is new," she said, a soft smile on her lips.

"What is?"

"You coming to pay a visit."

Shadow didn't consider himself the possessive or protective type, and yet he'd completely dominated Riley's world. If she moved, he knew about it. Her privacy was completely gone, she simply didn't know it yet.

Not that she'd ever know it.

This was a big mistake. Asking her for a beer.

Taking care of her, getting to know her. It left a trail of evidence to who he was. Even as he knew it was a mistake and should be doing everything to leave, he couldn't bring himself to do it.

She made him … want. He wanted the fantasy, wanted Riley. How was it possible to go so long without realizing he was missing something?

"I'm sorry," she said, startling him.

"Sorry?"

"You know, for today. I was a total bitch to you. I shouldn't have been. You were helping me, and I wasn't exactly the nicest person to be around," she said. "You could have been hurt."

"You watched me kill someone, and I don't know if I'm happy that you're not freaking out," he said.

She chuckled, actually chuckled. He couldn't believe it.

"You said it wasn't the worst thing you'd seen."

"We've gone over this," she said. "You know I was on the streets between foster care. I don't want to talk about that time. I don't even think about it."

"The cops, they were never on your side?"

"Some of them were okay. Others liked to give protection for a price. You can imagine what that price would be."

Sex. It was the same old shit. He didn't like it.

She smiled, and he found it to be such a sad one. He wanted to make her smile and for it to be real. Riley didn't realize just how familiar he was with her sadness.

"I'm sorry you had to go through that."

"It wasn't so bad. I got street smart real fast. Others weren't so lucky. They thought putting out would give them a better life. I was able to get by on my own." She took a sip of her beer, and he couldn't look away.

This woman was a fighter. She was strong, fierce,

and determined. There was so much to admire about her, and of course, she was attracted to him, which was kind of funny.

"The gym you caught me going to," he said. He may as well give her a little truth. "I work out there. A lot, actually. It's got its fair share of broken kids. I'm trying to … mentor a few of them. To show them there's another way. Violence isn't always the answer."

"Maybe it is."

He looked at her, and she stared intently back at him. Her eyes were so green, even in the dim backyard lighting. "It shouldn't have to be."

"Just because we don't want it to be, doesn't mean it's not. Some of the guys were determined to hurt me, to make me afraid. They used violence to try and control me. I used violence to show them I'm not to be messed with." She looked down at her bottle. "Don't take this personally, but violence seems to be part of your life. I'm pretty sure the guys around here couldn't handle a knife or a gun the way you did. Why are you living in the suburbs?"

He wasn't offended. Violence *was* his life. He was a contracted killer. Someone designed to take a life without asking a single question.

"I like the fakeness," he said. "I don't think that's even a real word." He blew out a breath. "Every single person on this street has something to hide, but it's the American dream. It's nice to blend into a crowd. To be normal."

She laughed. "You don't blend, Shadow. Every person sees you, and there's no getting away from that."

"Before you started snooping into my life, I went by undetected quite well."

"I've looked bullshit in the face one too many times. You've got it all over you." She held her hand out, pointing at his body. "I get it, though. We're not part of this world. They can laugh with each other and in the next breath, stab each other in the back. I've never been a fan of that kind of crap. It's a good thing what you're doing—trying to show those kids another way. The world needs more of that. Most of the time they get pushed to one side, and no one gives a crap about them."

He stared at her and knew no one had taken that time with her. She'd been alone in this world. Never part of it, and yet sucked into it by everyone else.

"You're not alone anymore," he said.

"I'm always alone, Shadow." She finished her beer, and handed him back the bottle. "I need to get some rest. Thank you for the drink and the company."

She went to walk away, but Shadow wasn't ready for her to be gone. Reaching out, he snagged her wrist, stopping her from going anywhere.

Riley didn't put up a fight with him. She waited for him to release her.

Standing up, he stepped close to her body. He felt such a rush, a desire he'd never experienced before. She tilted her head back to look at him, and for the longest time, he just stared.

Silence had always been a comfort to him. He could think, plan, and do anything that he put his mind to.

The interest in her gaze was still there. She wanted him, but was holding back.

He was making a mistake. Every second that he was with her, was a second longer than he should be. His life came with a use by date. There were people who'd hunt him down and kill him for the title of being the one to do it.

"Lock your door," he said. "If you need anything at all, I'll be here."

She nodded. Her lips looked so tempting. He

wanted to kiss her.

Would it be wrong to give in just this once and to take what he wanted? One kiss and then a second. A fuck, making love, falling in love. It would all happen. Riley had the power to make herself his weakness, and he couldn't have that. No way. He couldn't have that at all. He didn't want to do that to her.

"Good night." He pulled away, wanting to turn back and kiss those fuckable lips. He didn't though.

After getting back home he went straight to the basement. Clicking on the screens, he saw her standing at her backdoor. She had her fingers to her lips.

Had she been imagining it, too?

Get your head out of your ass!

Boss had given him a job, and he needed to stop thinking about his sexy little neighbor, and focus on the job at hand.

Even as he berated himself, he couldn't look away, nor could he turn the computer screen off. In that moment, leaning against the door, she looked so vulnerable. Everyone else in her world had walked all over her, taken advantage and not given a shit about her. Was it so wrong to want to be the only person who was different for her?

Chapter Five

Shadow leaned back on the worn leather sofa. The place reeked of a high school locker room, stale donuts, and cheap coffee. Normally he handled his business with Maurice by phone or text, but his assignment was proving to be more complicated than he hoped.

"He's had facial surgery, and I've already counted over a dozen body doubles," said Maurice from his chair in front of the keyboard.

"We already know this," said Shadow. He'd been doing recon on his mark for weeks, but the asshole was always one step ahead. Last night, Shadow had come seconds from pulling the trigger on a look-alike, only to discover it was another cold trail. It was too close of a call for his taste. "I need something I can use. Something that'll give away the real target. Boss doesn't want any mistakes."

"Like what?"

"I don't know. *Fuck.* Tattoo, birthmark, something the doubles won't have. I need to be one hundred percent certain before I blow his bastard's brains to kingdom come."

Maurice adjusted his glasses as hundreds of pics flashed across the numerous screens. "Give me a minute."

Shadow tapped his foot. He was impatient about getting this job done, but also couldn't get Riley off his mind. Since she barged into his life, he'd been slowly torn down the middle, his two worlds colliding. He needed his life at Killer of Kings—it was all he knew, and it kept the demons at bay.

Then there was *her.*

His carefully crafted veneer of normalcy helped him experience everything he'd lost, a life forever out of reach. He remembered the simplicity of having a drink with Riley under the stars. He could fall hard for a girl like her. As fucked up as it was, he already envisioned a future with his nosy little neighbor. They could play out all the fucking fairy tales, and scrub the past from their memories.

Only Shadow knew better. There was no going back, no happily ever after.

"You know Boss has me do a thorough background check on all his staff, right?"

Shadow narrowed his eyes, leaning over to rest his elbows on his knees. "What are you trying to say, Maurice?"

"Some of the reports say you're a sociopath. That you have an attachment disorder so severe that you can't function in normal society. Others call it PTSD."

He ground his teeth. "Why are you telling me this?"

"Boss thinks you're getting too close to one of your neighbors."

"My personal life is none of Boss's business. Or yours," he said. "How about you do your fucking job and leave my past where it belongs? If you haven't noticed, it's been a long time since I was a little boy at the mercy of the system."

His blood pressure rose to the point he could only hear his heart pounding in his ears. He usually kept his cool, but his past still managed to piss on his life and warp his thoughts. Shadow had been forced to watch his mother's health deteriorate for years. Even in those final months, she refused to get medical help. Holed up in their tiny apartment, in the seediest part of the city, it had been just the two of them. When things got desperate, he resorted to stealing to bring food home. And painkillers. And cigarettes. He'd only been nine years old.

Then the years of foster care. The brutal beatings, the starvation, the lack of any affection. He'd gone through all the stages of hell until there was nothing left but emptiness.

He survived on the streets from thirteen onward, another miserable chapter of his fucked-up life. The more he reflected, the more his muscles tensed. When Maurice cleared his throat, Shadow realized his hands were in tight fists, his knuckles turned white.

"I just wanted to say that a report can't define you. Sometimes they're not worth the paper they're written on." Maurice gave him a little smile, then turned back to the monitors. "Ah, there we go."

Maurice expanded an image. It was a small, insignificant tattoo in the web of his target's thumb and first finger.

"What is it?" Shadow asked.

"Looks like the infinity symbol."

"What a piece of shit. Are you sure it's on the original? None of his doubles have it?"

"I'm sure, Shadow. This is what I do all day. Every day."

He nodded, still reflecting on Maurice's words. Shadow had always believed the poison the social workers fed him. It was one of the reasons he kept to himself, convinced he was a monster. Maurice's declaration made him think.

"Why'd you mention that stuff about my reports, anyway?"

"Look, Shadow, I know all the dark stuff, from the foster system to your tours of duty. But, I also know what you do Thursday nights. I know about the shooting at the bar. You think you're the devil? The devil doesn't care about anyone but himself."

He stood up, tucking the 9mm on the coffee table

in the back of his pants. "Thanks for the information." Then he got up to leave, his hand on the door handle. "Boss give any contracts on the girl?"

"No, but Killian's his right-hand man these days."

"Take care of yourself," said Shadow, leaving the apartment. Once outside in the hallway, he leaned against the wall and scrubbed his hands over his face. He lived by himself and stayed away from other people to avoid this type of emotional overload. His memories were weaknesses he didn't need to relive.

At least Riley was safe for now. Maurice was right—if Killian found out Boss put a hit out on an innocent woman, there'd be hell to pay.

He headed out to the downtown core. According to his recon, the target had an appointment with a banker at 3:00, but it could be more smoke and mirrors. Shadow sat in his SUV and watched the entrance of the bank with his binoculars. As boredom settled in, he massaged behind his neck with one hand and checked his Rolex. A couple minutes to three, two cars pulled up in front. He waited to see who would step out after the rear passenger door was held open. When he spotted Chains driving the lead car, he tossed his binoculars and bolted from his vehicle.

Did Boss have more than one guy on the job or was Chains backstabbing Killer of Kings? Either way, his day just got more fucked up. He called Boss on his cell as he walked along the sidewalk, weaving in and out of suits. Shadow hated crowds.

"You finished the job early?" asked Boss.

"Good one. Since you have your finger on the pulse of the city, you know the answer. What *I* need to know is why Chains is driving around with my mark."

"I don't remember saying it was exclusive."

Shadow growled his irritation. "He's going to

blow his cover if he makes a move on the wrong guy. Maurice said he has a fucking army of body doubles."

"Chain is infiltrating on the down low. Nothing to do with your mark. I like to have eyes and ears everywhere. Just worry about getting your contract fulfilled."

"I'm on it."

Shadow shut off his phone and shoved it in his pocket. He had to get close enough to see the tattoo before he could take out his mark. It wouldn't be easy. As he approached the two idling cars, he glared at Chains, sitting in the driver's seat. He'd only worked with Chains briefly while they were handling the Dead Angels MC clean-up, but Shadow preferred to work alone.

He discreetly pressed a tracker to the rear of both vehicles before walking toward the bank. Shadow blended into the surroundings. Today, he'd dressed the part, wearing the tailored Brioni suit he saved for knocking off upscale bastards. The five men flanking his target were on alert, so he couldn't get close. With the security cameras and armed guards, he wouldn't be pulling out his guns inside the bank. He just needed to verify he had the right man, and then he'd follow the piece of shit outside of the city and take out all six of them.

Shadow had complete faith in his ability to get the job done, no matter how many fuckers he had to take down. Boss had taught him well. Firsthand experience at Killer of Kings over the last twenty years had put him at the top of his game.

The foyer of the historic bank was massive, the vaulting ceilings reminiscent of the museums in Rome. The marble floors shined with a mirror finish. Shadow had traveled the world on assignments, and spoke several languages. Italy had been one of his favorites.

He took out his phone, keeping tabs on the group while trying to look occupied. Shadow discreetly took pics of the men in the entourage. His mark had dirty-blond hair and looked to be in his mid-thirties. He'd expected someone much older considering how far his criminal enterprise reached. Didn't matter. It was either him or a double, and Shadow was getting fucking sick of recon.

Maybe shaking things up would bring the real man to the surface … or send him deeper into hiding. He had to do this one right, just as Boss instructed. He liked assignments that were cut and dry—find and eliminate the mark without all this bullshit. Maybe Boss was punishing him for his last fuck-up.

"You clean up well." The voice came from directly behind him. As much as he'd love to whirl around and shove his Glock in the asshole's face, he kept still.

"Don't get excited. I'm not into dudes," said Shadow before he turned partly to the side.

He frowned when he saw Anthony DeVino, one of the mob's low-ranking hitmen. Shadow should have expected competition with such a high payout.

"What? Not happy to see me?"

"You reek of cold cuts and cigars, not exactly a pleasant combination." Shadow put his phone away, occasionally keeping tabs on his mark as he crossed his arms. "Give me some space."

"You're breakin' my heart here, Shadow."

"What do you want?"

Anthony shrugged, but glanced to the other end of the foyer. "I'm guessing the same as you."

"Then we have nothing else to say, do we?" said Shadow.

Anthony stayed quiet for a shocking ten seconds.

"Boss doesn't own the city."

"And Renzo Carpollo does? Keep telling yourself that, DeVino. *Usa la testa, vai a casa.*" If he had to take out Anthony to fulfill this contract, he wouldn't think twice. Killer of Kings considered him a scavenger, always ready to pick up the scraps left by real hitmen.

Shadow headed to the main entrance, each step punctuated on the stone floor. He waited on the stairs outside, hoping to get a good look at the mystery man as he left. He couldn't stop thinking about Riley's lip-reading skill. If he could understand what they were saying across the foyer, it could be a game changer. It would save him a lot of time and recon. He liked to work solo, and didn't want to drag around one of Boss's hired lip-readers to every lead. If he needed one, he knew exactly who he'd use—Riley. He enjoyed watching her, and being around her, even if at times she was a bit prickly.

He paced along the wide stairs, occasionally checking his watch. When he heard voices approaching, he left a wide berth of space at the entrance. Two bodyguards came out first, followed by the blond and the three other guards. Shadow moved in closer, pretending to absently talk on his phone.

They moved too fast for him to see the guy's hand. The odds of seeing the small tattoo was slim to none to start with. Normally, he'd follow and kill them anyway. If it was the wrong guy, he'd keep hunting. Since Boss wanted this hit to be perfect, with nothing done to alert the target, he had to bide his time.

****

Shadow had been MIA for almost two weeks. It drove her crazy. Not because she hadn't seen him, but because she couldn't stop obsessing over him. Riley prided herself on keeping her heart locked up tight. It was better that way.

Shadow complicated everything.

She refused to knock on his door and look desperate. If he wanted to see her, he knew where she lived and worked. It would have been easier to put him out of her head if she hadn't believed there'd been something building between them. Had she been completely wrong? Maybe he was just a nice guy, a neighbor looking out for her. Maybe she'd imagined everything else—the intimacy, the possessiveness, the way he looked at her. God, she wanted to believe a man like Shadow could fall for her. But like the rest of her life, it looked like it would end in more disappointment.

After work, she locked up her bakery and headed to her car. She noticed that ever since the "incident", the area near her bakery was unusually clear of parked cars. It was odd. Of course, she couldn't get that day out of her head. Not because Shadow killed a man, but because he'd done it for her. He literally killed for her. And now he was gone.

She started up her car, and then rolled down the windows. Even the evenings were humid at this time of year.

"No more broken windows?"

Riley gasped. Shadow's hand was on the roof of her car, his face distractingly close. "Um, no. Everything's been good."

He nodded. "I'm glad."

The only place opened at this hour was the variety store and the bar. She hoped he'd been there to see her, but wasn't going to hold her breath. "I hope you weren't here for baked goods. I closed shop a while ago."

"I'm here for you."

Her heart melted, but she kept up a collected front. "Oh?"

"I want to take you out to dinner, Riley."

Her name on his lips sent butterflies rushing to her womb. This was the last thing she expected from Mr. MIA. She became tongue-tied, part of her expecting him to be playing a cruel trick on her. Riley played along. "When?"

"Tonight. I'll pick you up in an hour." He stared at her with those dark, haunted eyes. The man was completely confident. Why shouldn't he be?

She chuckled. "Are you being serious?"

He winked. "Wear something nice. It's fine dining."

Then he stood straight and walked off.

What the actual fuck?

She tried to wrap her mind around what just happened. Shadow wanted to take her to dinner? Fine dining? Riley didn't even think she owned a nice dress. She had an hour to get showered and dressed, so she made haste getting out of the plaza.

It was nearly eight o'clock by the time she was ready. Clothes littered her bedroom floor. She'd tried on just about her whole wardrobe, but guessed she couldn't go wrong with a little black dress. After doing her hair and makeup, she dug out her heels from the back of the closet. Riley wasn't a high maintenance girl. She couldn't even remember the last time she'd worn heels or lipstick.

She did a twirl in front of the hall mirror, trying to envision what Shadow would see when he showed up at her door. Riley smiled. It was fun getting dressed up, and she was happy with the final outcome.

When a loud, hollow knocking echoed in her little bungalow, Riley froze in place. She'd half expected him to be a no-show.

She opened the door and stared at Shadow. He wore a full suit, his dark hair slicked back. The man looked good enough to eat.

"You look stunning," he said, his voice rough and smooth at the same time.

"Thank you," she said. "I don't have many fancy dresses."

He wet his thick lips, and she couldn't look away. "You're perfect." The way he said the words left no room for argument. He reached out his hand and she took it.

Soon after locking up, they were in his car, the soft leather caressing her thighs.

"I never see you drive this car," she said.

"It's for special occasions."

She breathed in his subtle cologne, a mix of musk and sandalwood. His hands on the steering wheel were big and strong, his fingers long with neatly trimmed nails. She noticed little details about people, and the oddest things seemed to turn her on.

"I haven't seen you around for weeks," she said, being nosy. He hadn't even put out his garbage.

The hum of the engine picked up as he sped down the highway. "I've been working a lot. My current assignment has been a challenge."

"Investments, right?"

"Right."

She bit her lip, wanting to know more about Shadow, but not wanting to pry. He'd asked her to dinner, so her previous assumption that they had a connection must have been right. Sooner or later, he had to open up.

"I haven't had any more trouble at the plaza," she said. "I was scared they'd try and retaliate or get the police involved." Riley still couldn't understand how murder could be swept under the rug.

He flicked his wrist to adjust his watch, his eyes on the road. "I dealt with them. It won't be a problem."

What did that mean? Was that why no one from the bar dared park near her bakery? The mere thought that Shadow had that much weight gave her a little rush. It definitely turned her on to be with such a capable man. He made her feel safe, and that was something she'd lacked most of her life.

The inside of the car was too quiet. She shifted and watched the darkened scenery rush by, and her thoughts drifted. Riley remembered the day she'd been taken into police protective custody, the beginning of her foster care nightmare. The cops had given her a yellow knitted monkey, a small consolation for what was to come.

That wasn't the day she'd lost her sense of safety, though. That had ended before she could remember. Being born to an addict was a special kind of hell. The nauseating rollercoaster ride ended when her mother tried to sell her for one night of fucking to an undercover agent in exchange for drugs. She'd been twelve. Although she'd been spared that trauma, her childhood innocence had been lost amongst layers of dysfunction she desperately wanted to wipe from memory.

Even as an adult, she never looked up her mother. Why would she? Riley only had herself to rely on, and that's how she liked it.

"We're here." Shadow's voice snapped her out of her reverie.

She looked around, the lights and glitter of a massive archway now catching her attention. It was fine dining to the tenth degree. A valet opened her door, and she stepped out, feeling awkward with such luxuries.

A long line-up of people stood behind a red velvet rope, a bouncer keeping them back, but Shadow appeared and led her up the steps ahead of everyone. She felt like Cinderella, in more ways than one.

"This is way too fancy," she whispered.

Shadow led her inside where he followed the hostess to their table. "This is the one I requested?" he asked.

"It is, sir."

He held out her chair, and she sat down, watching the flames of the candle flicker when her foot nudged the table leg. To her right, she heard live piano and violin.

Shadow sat across from her. "Thank you for coming on such short notice."

"I was just surprised since you disappeared after that night in my backyard."

"My work is complicated, but I promise I'd rather be with you," he said.

She smiled. "No offense, but I tend to be skeptical. I haven't exactly had good experience with men."

"I have no reason to lie." His eyes were deep pools she could get lost in, and she craved to know every secret.

"Then tell me something about yourself. Everything about you is a mystery. I want to know the real you."

"You don't want to know him."

Riley tilted her head. "Of course I do," she said. She thought of something to ask. "How did you get the name *Shadow*?"

He paused, then slowly bit his lower lip. "It's just a name."

"Did your mother give it to you?" Why was he so afraid to open up to her? It seemed she finally met someone more secretive than she was.

The waitress came with water. Shadow immediately grabbed his glass and took a drink. "My boss gave it to me. A long time ago."

"It suits you." She didn't pry further on the subject, but she wasn't done with him. "Have you been married before?"

This question didn't seem to upset him like the other. In fact, he smirked, a deliciously sexy tilt of the lips. "No, I haven't been married."

"Children?"

He shook his head, then looked at his menu. She decided to look at hers, only to find it was in French. When she glanced over at him, he had the same devilish smirk.

"Need help?" he asked.

"Maybe a little. I'm not interested in eating snails or duck liver."

The waitress returned to see if they needed help with their order. Shadow spoke in fluent French, which surprised her. "Did you want a glass of wine?" he asked her.

"Sure. Whatever you're having."

When the waitress left, she leaned over the table. "Are you French?"

"Just a language I picked up. I travel a lot for work."

"I've never been out of this state."

"Never traveled?"

Riley shook her head. Now that she thought of it, there weren't many boxes checked off on her bucket list, but at least she had her bakery, and that was a big one. She didn't need bright lights and luxury vacations.

"There are so many places I'd love to show you," he said. "Maybe I will one day."

All she'd ever wanted was a simple life. She'd expected to live it alone, but now she craved so much more … thanks to the man sitting across from her. Riley was terrified to get her hopes up, only to have them dashed. "Girls like me learn to let go of dreams. There's no disappointment that way."

"Don't say that," he said. He reached his arm across the table and held her wrist, and she held his. "Have big dreams. You deserve them." With his free hand, he ran the backs of his fingers along her cheek. She closed her eyes, savoring this new level of intimacy.

When he abruptly pulled away, she swallowed hard and adjusted her dress. She'd completely fallen under his spell for those few minutes.

Shadow stared at another table, completely focused on the people being seated. "Riley, can you do me a favor?"

"Okay…" She supposed she owned him a lot of favors after the glass repair.

"Don't look now, but I need you to read the lips at that table."

Chapter Six

Shadow didn't like using Riley, but at least he had an excuse to take her out to dinner. She looked so beautiful, and she had literally taken his breath away. For a split second he'd felt a little guilty that he was using her for his own means.

He believed the man currently having a business meal was his target, but he wanted to be one hundred percent sure.

Reading lips wasn't his skill, but he knew without a doubt that it was Riley's. She was an expert at it.

She glanced over at the table, and he stared at her neck. How would she react if he was to press his lips to her pulse? Would she shiver, and beg for more? Maybe kick him in the balls and tell him to fuck off? Or would she turn toward him and kiss him back?

He couldn't get her out of his mind, and it was driving him crazy.

With the security cameras he had in her home, he knew what she looked like naked, and he liked what he saw. Nice big juicy tits, full ass and thighs. There was not a thing he didn't like about her or her body.

She was intrigued by him, and damn nosy, but did that extend to physical attraction? Riley played her cards against her chest, and he didn't have a clue where he stood. He wasn't the typical playboy women flocked to. Most kept their distance.

"Why?" she asked.

"What?"

She frowned. "Why do you want me to read their lips?"

"Because I'm curious."

"Does this have to do with your job?" she asked.

"Yes."

She pursed her lips, and glanced back over at the table. "What do I get out of this?" she asked.

He sat back and stared at her. "You want something from me?"

"You want something from me, so I think it'll be good to get something in return."

Now he was intrigued. "What would you like, Riley?" If it was too much he'd turn it down. He could think of a lot of things he'd like to give her.

"An actual date where you don't want me for my mad skills," she said.

"This is a real date. It's classy."

"And I'm only here because you can't see what they're saying. Don't try to pretend that this is something else. I know it's not, and I'm not stupid." She pushed some of her hair back that had fallen over her eyes. "What's it going to be?"

Riley's request made him smile. She could have asked him for anything, and yet all she wished for was an actual date. What was is about this woman that managed to melt his cold exterior?

"Fine. I'll take you out for a date. A real date. Now tell me what they're saying," he said. Shadow didn't want to fuck up this intel. If this was his man, he needed to know.

She took a sip of her wine, and he watched as she rested her head on her hand to glance over. To any onlooker, she was simply observing the table.

He stared at her. He couldn't help himself, and when she glanced over, she snorted. "You could help me along and pretend to be an awful date."

Shadow was confused.

Riley rolled her eyes. "Are you for real? You want to know what they're saying, and clearly you don't want them to know what I'm doing. Look at your phone.

Pretend to be a bad date that is more interested in other details than me."

"Oh, right, of course." He was totally fucking this up.

The fact of the matter was, he liked watching her. Riley intrigued him, and now she was ruining his renowned attention to detail.

Grabbing his cell phone, he began to text Maurice, and then Boss. It was useless shit. A date, time, and even some emojis, which was just funny. He even texted Viper while he was at it.

"Okay, they're talking about a date. He's got to head out of the city. Someone's following him. He knows they're getting close." There was a pause. "They're talking about a hit. They know there's a hit out and he's being advised on going under the knife again."

Out of the corner of his eye, he saw her tense up.

"What else?" he asked.

"Something about a distinguishing mark. A tattoo that he needs to get rid of." She looked toward him for a second, and he didn't like how focused she was. "A hit. Okay, I know my movies and a hit in the movies means a kill, right? Murder? He's part of your job, but you said you deal with investments. Are you really a hitman?"

Shadow stared at her.

Time ticked by, and still he couldn't find words.

"That's it, isn't it? That's your big secret. You're a hitman, and you're on assignment. This is just another clue. Not to mention that nasty looking guy you were talking with the other week. Then of course your skills with a knife and a gun. You've got something about you that screams you're a man who can take care of himself."

He folded his arms, and waited for the freak out. Getting close to a civilian was a fucked-up idea, and he knew better.

Riley grabbed her wine, and took another sip. "Well? What is it going to be? The truth or another lie."

Silence fell between them.

Shadow had never dealt with a situation like this, and he didn't know what the hell to do. Gritting his teeth, he looked around the restaurant, wishing he could find the right words.

"You know what, deal with this shit on your own." She threw down her napkin, and glared at him.

He watched her stomp off, and he waved the waiter over. Shadow rushed through paying just as Riley tripped, falling into the man that he was investigating.

Fuck!

He tensed up as Chains entered the restaurant. There was no way for him to help Riley. He also didn't want to risk Chains seeing him.

Killer of Kings wasn't an exclusive company, and any of the members could do whatever the hell they wanted, including taking other contracts. Chains was not obliged to stick it out with Boss.

Shadow had no choice but to use the bathroom, and to actually find an exit that didn't put him into contact with anyone. Within ten minutes he was out on the street, checking left and right as his car was brought around.

After paying the valet, he climbed behind the wheel, and began driving away, keeping his gaze on the streets. He didn't like Riley being alone, even if she was in a public place.

Their date hadn't gone well at all. A love life just wasn't in the cards for a man like him. Allowing himself to hope for more was like chasing the wind.

Pulling around the first sharp bend, just ahead, he saw Riley resting against the wall, her arms folded.

He slowed down to a stop, and she came to the

car, climbing into the passenger side without a word.

"What the hell was that all about?" he asked.

Shadow was so pissed. Not only could she have gotten hurt, she'd fucked up days of grueling intel.

"You didn't want to have dinner with me. All you wanted was to find out what that guy was all about."

He heard the disappointment in her voice, and it hit him like a punch to the gut. Shadow wasn't used to caring. Damn it, he shouldn't feel bad about using her.

Driving for a couple of minutes, he tried to think of what to say. "I'm sorry."

"No, you're not."

"I am. Don't even bother trying to tell me what I'm thinking and not thinking. I wanted to have dinner with you. You're wrong about me. I enjoyed our time together."

He glanced over at her, and saw her watching him. She had big, expressive eyes, a sweet innocent air about her. He was falling down the fucking rabbit hole and couldn't get out now if he tried.

"So ... you don't want this?"

Shadow saw she held a cell phone in her hands.

"Your cell phone?"

She chuckled. "This isn't mine. This is your guy's phone. When I tripped, I took it from him. Take it."

He reached out, and took hold of the phone. Even as he drove, he flicked it open, and saw there was a code to get inside.

It wouldn't be hard to break, but it would take time. Pocketing the cell phone, the rest of the drive was in silence.

She was completely weird. There was no other word for it.

After her question about him being a hitman, he'd thought she'd run from him, but she didn't. Instead, she'd gone and gotten him the cell phone that would tell him if this was his guy. He'd known it was after the lip reading, and it wouldn't be long now until his mission was done.

He parked onto his driveway, and as he turned off the ignition, Riley was already out of the car, and inside her own home.

Shadow didn't stop her. He exhaled in defeat, and got out of the car.

Tonight had been a total fuck up, and there was no getting back from it.

Entering his home, he already knew that Boss was there waiting for him. Shadow closed his door, and went straight to his kitchen, grabbing a beer.

"Do you have any idea how much danger she was in tonight?" Boss asked.

Shadow twisted off the cap, and took a long swig. He didn't want to deal with this man tonight.

His neighbor was the only person on his mind. She had gotten under his skin even though he'd tried to stop it. Even arguing with her entertained him. There was something inexplicable about that hot little number.

Grabbing the cell phone out of his pocket, he slapped it on the counter, and slid it over to Boss. "There you go. Get it to Maurice and tell me if I'm onto the right guy."

"This is *your* job."

Finally, Shadow turned to look at Boss. His eyes were black, like a cobra's, impossible to read. "You're not here to take the job from me?"

"No. Actually, I came to tell you that Viper, Bain, and Killian have been able to have a life that fits with them at Killer of Kings, even with their families."

He narrowed his eyes. Boss didn't do nice. "Are you trying to tell me to have a relationship?" Shadow asked.

"I wouldn't dream of it." Boss winked.

"She knows what I am."

"And yet she didn't run away from you screaming. I think you've got to think about that. She sounds like a good fit." Boss tapped the cell phone. "Use your head, Shadow."

He watched as Boss left his home leaving him with more questions than answers.

Grabbing the cell phone, he headed downstairs toward the computers.

It wouldn't take long for his hit to realize that his cell phone was gone. From then it would lead back to Riley.

She didn't even realize that she'd put her life at risk to help him. And he'd been a fool to involve her. She knew a lot, and Boss didn't like any kind of exposure for the organization.

Firing up the computers, he watched Riley remove the dress she'd worn. Her hair cascaded down her back, and the black lingerie looked so damn tempting.

She sat on the end of the bed with her head in her hands.

Seeing her like that, almost as if she was giving up, he didn't like that. Not at all.

There was a fire inside of Riley, and he'd ruined that. He'd made her feel disposable.

No, he couldn't let that happen.

Shadow rushed from his house, and he used the spare key that he'd made for himself, and let himself through her front door.

He'd broken so many rules with Riley, letting her know his name, and a lot of other personal things about him, but he wasn't about to change that, he couldn't.

Locking her door, he walked up her stairs, and then paused.

What the hell was he doing?

She didn't want to see him right now.

Give her the truth.

She'd seen him kill a man and didn't freak out. Surely, she'd be able to handle whatever he could say.

Shadow opened her bedroom door and leaned against the doorframe, folding his arms.

"Do I even want to know why you're here? Or how you got in?"

His first thought was to lie. To tell her she left the door open, but he was tired of all the lies and half-truths. "I have a key." He lifted it up and showed it to her.

"Of course you do. You have a key." She glanced down at her body and shrugged. She was still in her black lingerie, but she didn't make any move to hide her body. Riley had no spark.

Shadow couldn't stop looking at her. Even in her defeated state, she was exquisite and far sexier close up than in the view of the monitors.

His cock thickened, and all he could think about was fucking her. She looked beautiful and vulnerable at the same time.

She stood up and glared at him. Without her heels, there was no way for her to match him in height.

"You know, this world is one shitty fucked up place. I've seen a lot of things in my time already." She stopped, licking her lips. "Maybe one day you'll see you're not alone in it."

She went to move away, and he should let her. Shadow knew that deep down in his heart this didn't end well. This ended in death and fire, and evil. Still, he reached out, clasping her wrist, sentencing them as he did so. How could it not? She was an innocent. He didn't care what she said. She may have seen evil, but the truth was, he'd seen hell on earth.

Together, they wouldn't help each other.

They couldn't.

Too many obstacles were in their way, and yet, he pulled her close. Almost as if it was an out of body experience, he held her waist. There was no stopping him now. He couldn't stop, nor did he want to.

The feel of her skin beneath his hand was perfect, so warm and soft.

Staring into her eyes, he couldn't look away. He cupped her cheek, running his thumb across her lips. Such tempting lips, begging to be kissed.

"I'll tell you everything, but first I've got to have a little taste."

Before she could say another word, he claimed her lips.

****

This couldn't be happening.

Riley moaned as Shadow's tongue traced across her lips, and she opened her mouth, tasting him for the first time. Their kiss started tentatively, their tongues mingling until the hunger for more took over. She'd been so angry with him, hated him even, and yet she couldn't think of a single reason why he shouldn't be kissing her, or why she shouldn't be kissing him back. Knowing he wanted her was addictive, making her soar.

Grabbing onto his arms, she pressed herself closer against him, whimpering as both his hands cupped her ass.

It felt so damn good to be in his strong arms, and even as she wanted to fight it, her pussy flooded with warmth. She wanted him, craved him, needed him. Her body was desperate for this man, had been for the longest time.

He was her drug of choice, and she didn't want to quit.

One of his hands moved from her ass, and slid up her back, sinking into her hair, holding her close. He was rough and attentive, making her drift from reality.

Shadow hulked over her, making her feel small and feminine.

She released his arms and slid her hands inside his jacket, pushing it off. Next, she worked on the buttons of his shirt, opening each one. She could only imagine what he looked like naked, and in fact she *had* imagined it many lonely nights.

He didn't make a move to help her, or to rid her own body of her lingerie. He stood there, allowing her to undress him. The man was patient and deadly, which only turned her on more. Pushing the shirt over his broad shoulders, he stopped her progress by claiming another kiss.

Shadow pressed her against the wall, and trapped her there with his rock-hard body.

"Now you're my captive." He took hold of her hands, pinning them above her head, turning her on even more.

"Yes, I'm your captive. What are you going to do with me?"

He kept her hands locked together above her head, and with his other hand, he trailed a path down her body until he cupped her breast.

The lace didn't hide a thing. Her nipple puckered against his palm, and she bit her lip as he pinched the hardened tip.

"I'm going to fuck you until you can't think straight, and you're going to let me."

She chuckled. "I'm not fighting you."

This time he smiled, a delicious tilt of the lips. "No, you're not."

He released the clasp of her bra, and her breasts

tumbled out. The bra still clung to her body, but gave him enough access to play with her breasts. "These are a thing of beauty." He pinched the rough tips, making her cry out.

The pleasure went straight to her clit even as it mingled with a little pain.

"Are you wet for me, baby?" he asked.

"Yes." There was no point in lying to him. She'd never been so ready in her life.

She was soaking, and with each touch of his hand, she was getting wetter.

No man had ever made her feel like this, so consumed with passion that she couldn't think straight. Riley was so desperate for Shadow, she was ready to beg.

From the very beginning, he'd taken control of her thoughts, just by being mysterious. That had only gotten stronger as she got to know him.

She wanted him more than anything else, every bit, good and bad. Riley wanted to be taken by the hitman.

He bent his head, and she gasped as he took one of her nipples into his mouth, sucking hard. The pain mingling with the pleasure drove her crazy. She didn't know if she should push him away, or hold him closer.

She pressed her thighs together, wanting some friction on her clit.

"No, that's mine." Shadow pressed her thighs open by sliding his leg between hers.

Her pussy pressed against his covered thigh as he was still wearing pants.

She let out a little gasp as the movement of his leg sent a shockwave of need rushing through her. He was going to drive her crazy if she wasn't careful.

Finally, after what seemed like ages, he released her hands. In the next second, he lifted her up, and placed her on the bed, spreading her legs as he did. He looked like a sentry standing at the foot of her bed, staring down with an intense need in his eyes. Shadow tossed his shirt, and even in the darkness, she could see his upper body covered in wicked ink. This was no ordinary neighbor. He was the devil, a beautiful beast that was going to change her life.

She lifted up onto her elbows and watched as he knelt down at the edge, and then his lips were on her pussy. She tossed her head back, shocked by how take charge this man was.

He circled her clit with his hot tongue, flicking back and forth, creating a rush of arousal. She was so wet that she knew she had to be soaking the bed. She felt a trickle leak out, and tease over her anus.

"You taste so fucking good." He plunged his tongue deep inside her, and she cried out as he drew his tongue up, and circled her clit. "I want you to come all over my tongue, Riley. Come and scream my name."

She collapsed to the bed as he sucked on her clit, driving her close to her peak. It had been so long since she had been with anyone, and Shadow was a master. She didn't want to stop him, especially as she'd had so many fantasies of him doing exactly this.

Riley hoped that this time, she didn't wake up.

His fingers slid inside her. One, then two, and she gasped as he plunged them deep at the same time taking her clit into his mouth, and sucking hard. He ravaged her body, pulling her deeper into his web.

Closing her eyes, she allowed all of her troubles to ebb away so the only thing she focused on was the pleasure of his tongue. His hands worked like magic. How could one man have so much skill?

Shadow was relentless as he teased her clit, and the build toward her orgasm began. The sweet zone hovered close, and she began to pant, grabbing the sheets in her fists.

He stroked her pussy, taking her to heights that she'd never known.

She screamed his name as the powerful release washed over her, sending pleasure to every single nerve ending within her body. There was no stopping it, and Shadow didn't relent. He didn't stop at just one. He pushed her toward a second orgasm, and she was panting, gasping, needing so much more.

Shadow pulled away, and she sat up, a little shaken from what his mouth had done. She watched as he lowered the zipper of his pants.

Everything seemed to be in slow motion as he removed those pants followed by his boxer briefs.

He was rock hard, and his cock sprang out, the tip glistening with pre-cum. She couldn't help but lick her lips. The man was beyond impressive, an Adonis if she ever saw one. Those hours at the gym had paid off with interest.

She watched, mesmerized as he tore into a condom that he'd gotten out of his pants' pocket, and rolled the latex over his shaft.

Shadow moved toward her, and she finally glanced up to look at his face. The heat in his eyes made her start.

No one had ever looked at her like that. Not as if she was a morsel of food. She'd always been a quick lay, never something worth committing to. Shadow looked like he wanted to own her, and she loved that feeling of being wanted.

As he came toward her, he bent forward, cupping her face as he claimed her lips. Slowly, he moved her back so that she was laid out on the bed, and Shadow had followed her. Her legs were open, and when he broke from the kiss, she couldn't look away from his gaze.

He pressed the tip of his cock to her entrance, but he didn't look away from her either. Was he waiting for her to tell him to stop? Riley didn't know what he wanted. She knew what she craved, what she'd dreamt about for a long time now. God, she needed him inside her, needing him to quell the desperate ache.

In a single thrust, he slammed every inch of his dick inside her. Riley couldn't hold back the moan as he filled her pussy. It felt that good. He slid his hands beneath her head, holding her close, taking possession of her mouth as his cock pulsed deep within her.

He was big and she didn't know if the pressure was on the verge of pain or not, or because she hadn't been with anyone else for a long time.

Their kiss stirred something deep within. Something was happening here, something monumental. She felt connected to him on a soul deep level, and prayed it wasn't one-sided.

Shadow broke from the kiss, and she became lost in his intense stare. This man. He'd come into her life, and not willingly either. She'd made him take notice of her, and now she didn't want to get rid of him. She didn't care about his secrets. They all had them, and there was no getting away from it, nor did she want to.

Slowly, he began to rock inside her.

Making love, which shocked her as well.

"You have no idea what you do to me, do you?" he asked, his voice rough, deep, and hypnotic.

He pulled all of the way out of her, and she whimpered, not wanting him gone. Shadow didn't make her wait for long as he plundered inside her, going deeper than before. He released her head, and moved up so that he had leverage on his arms. She wrapped her legs around his waist, driving her pussy onto his dick. He rocked her body, fucking her like a beast, bringing her closer and closer to a new peak.

Shadow suddenly pulled out of her body, and with quick work, spun her over so that she was on her knees. He found her heat, and slammed all the way inside her, making her cry out.

"You feel so tight, so fucking perfect. I knew you would."

His hand cupped her stomach, and then slid down to stroke through her pussy. He found her clit, and began to tease her, driving her arousal for him higher.

She didn't think it was possible to find another release, but Shadow brought another from her, and she cried out as her orgasm washed over her once again.

Shadow cupped her hips, and slammed into her over and over. He filled her, driving deep, and moaned as his cock brought her toward another peak of pleasure.

She heard him groan as he filled her, and then felt the pulse of his cock as the orgasm filled the condom.

They were both panting, and Riley closed her eyes, a little shaken by what they had shared, and how quickly he'd taken over.

It felt like they'd been together hours, but it had all happened in a whirlwind. Pushing her hair off her face, she felt his hand go to her stomach as he moved over her. His lips grazed her skin, teasing the tendrils of hair at the back of her neck.

Even though she was completely exhausted, her neck was a highly erogenous zone. One little touch, and she was ready for more.

His lips touched her ear.

"You were right, Riley."

She tensed up as his words registered in her head.

"I'm a hitman, and you should never have let me fuck you."

Chapter Seven

Riley's eyes were still closed as she stretched out her legs in bed. She felt so comfortable, so completely sated. Then she tensed as her waking mind processed everything that had happened the night before.

I slept with my hot neighbor!

She peeked open her eyes, half wondering if she'd dreamt the whole thing. Shadow was asleep on her bed. Riley studied his back, the way it sloped down from his massive set of shoulders to his tapered waist. His skin was a light golden hue, and the closer she looked, the more she noticed the multitude of old scars. She wanted to run her fingers along those wounds, but didn't want to wake him.

Everything felt real in the light of day, reality snuffing out the fog of passion. Would he still feel the same way? Or had this always been about sex? Riley wasn't used to men sticking around or wanting to keep her forever. She refused to put down all her guards with Shadow until she was certain he wouldn't break her heart.

She remembered his warning from last night. He thought she'd made a mistake by sleeping with him. Riley wasn't afraid. She knew exactly what he was: a hitman, a killer for hire. If she was smart, she'd run the other way, but she'd never been one to follow the rules. And she wanted him. He was perfect—gorgeous, mysterious, damaged, and the man was a beast in bed. She'd been forced to survive on her own for most of her life, not relying on anyone. Refusing to rely on anyone. But it felt uniquely satisfying being with a man who could take care of her, protect her from anything or anybody. She was tired of fighting, tired of being alone.

Riley started to sit up when Shadow rolled to his back, one arm bent over his head on the pillow. He looked equally stunning and adorable first thing in the morning. In her bed. She dropped back down, holding the sheet over her nudity.

"Hey," she whispered.

"Morning, beautiful."

Immediately, she wondered what she looked like. Her hair and makeup would be a disaster. Regardless, the way he assessed her made her feel like the most sought-after woman in the world.

"About last night—"

"You want your key back?" he asked, giving her a cute smirk. He rolled to his side, facing her. With daylight coming in her window, she had a clear view of his elaborate tattoos and all those perfectly defined muscles. God, she wanted to touch him.

"You'd just make another," she teased. Riley dared to reach forward and trace her finger over one of the inked patterns on his pec. "Tell me about all this. About you," she said. "You're so secretive."

She felt a connection with Shadow, but there were so many layers yet to unravel. Riley didn't want this to end as a one-night stand.

"Comes with the territory," he said. His eyes were so dark, and he stared at her as if memorizing the colored flecks in her eyes. She loved how special he made her feel. He pushed up on an elbow and reached out, clutched her head behind the neck, bringing her in for a kiss. She closed her eyes and melted against his lips—the slow, sensual tease bringing her body to life. But she couldn't fall victim again, not when he was still a complete mystery to her.

"What territory?" asked, pulling back. "You seem to know a lot about me, but I don't know anything about you." She licked her lips, combing her fingers through her hair.

"Trust me, you know more than most." His muscles flexed as he attempted to lean forward to kiss her again. She pressed a hand to his chest to keep him at bay. Every cell in her body wanted to give in, to allow him to dominate her body again. But her heart and mind didn't want to be forgotten.

"I know you're a hitman. You work out at one of the sketchiest gyms I've ever seen. You put out your garbage the same time every week. That's about it," she said. Riley took a risk, praying it didn't push him away. "I want to know the real you. I want what happened between us to mean something."

He exhaled, a sound of defeat. "You were in the foster system. So was I," he said. "That was the start. That's when my childhood ended."

She nodded, not able to speak.

"It's been a rough ride, but we can't change the past," he said.

"Your parents?" Riley was terrified to push the wrong button, to make him close up on her. She knew all about memories, the type that weaseled their way into her nightmares. They were better left forgotten, but they still molded her into the person she was. She needed to know what made Shadow tick.

He clearly struggled for words, and she felt guilty for asking. Still, there couldn't be secrets and mysteries if they wanted more than a relationship consisting of quick dates and hot sex.

"I never met my father. My mother died when I was nine. There's no one else."

"How did she die?"

He narrowed his eyes. "You don't hold back, do you?"

She touched his cheek, running her fingers over his morning stubble. "I've never had anyone to talk to this way. Nobody ever understands or cares. You can talk to me, too."

"She had no family, no money. By the time she knew she was sick, she was too far gone. I took care of her, but I was just a fucking kid."

"I'm sorry," she said, her fingers still on his face. He grabbed her wrist and kissed her pulse point.

"The years of foster care were fucking brutal, but they still weren't worse than watching her die of lung cancer," he said. "She didn't live a good life, but she was my mother."

"You loved her," said Riley. "I can't even imagine what you went through."

"Her death taught me an important lesson," he said. "If you don't take care of yourself, you'll end up the same way. I'll never let that happen to me."

She trailed her fingers over his bicep, so hard and cut. "Is that why you work out so much?"

"One of the reasons. I need to keep my body strong—no drugs, no smoking, healthy living."

"Just because it happened to her, doesn't mean it will happen to you," she said. "You can't live your life in fear."

He smirked. "I'm not afraid to die, Riley. I risk my life every day in my line of work. I never assume I'll come home at night. I'm afraid to die the way she did: sick, helpless, pathetic, withering away to nothing knowing there's not a fucking thing anyone can do to change it."

She bit her bottom lip. For the first time since meeting him, she'd broken through. She could feel his pain, his sincerity, and she was falling in love.

"You are strong, Shadow." He'd opened up to her, and the new emotional bond was powerful. She wanted to erase all the pain, to heal him with her love.

Maybe he could do the same for her.

"Like you?"

She shrugged. "If we're being honest, I'm not as strong as I look. I've had to be since before I can remember. My mom wasn't a good woman. She was an addict, so far gone she was ready to sell *my* body for drugs. Foster care wasn't much better. I don't want pity or anything. I just want you to understand."

He kissed her forehead. "You'd make a great mother," he said. "You're nothing like her. You're smart, ambitious, and sweet."

Riley smiled. "Why have kids of my own when there are so many like us stuck in the foster system?"

"Makes sense. I know you could make a difference."

"Have you thought about kids?"

He pushed up onto his hands, looking down on her. "No more questions about me, baby girl. Tell me why you're alone, why there's no man in your life."

"Maybe I'm unlovable," she said.

"Come on, tell me…"

She swallowed hard. "I want it all, the whole happily ever after. The men I've dated wanted sex, not love. They wouldn't consider settling down with someone like me, anyway."

"Someone like you?"

Riley rolled her eyes. "I'm fat, Shadow. In case you haven't noticed. Men don't care about what you're like on the inside, not if the outside isn't perfect," she said. "I should be asking why *you've* been alone."

"Because I hadn't met you yet. And now that I have you, I'm never letting you go." He still had her hand pinned. Shadow used the strength in his arms to lower himself enough to kiss her neck. His tongue shelled her ear the sound of his breath soothing her. "You're perfect,

Riley. Fucking gorgeous and perfect."

"Kiss me," she said. "Please."

He released her wrist before brushing his lips against hers. She wrapped her arms around his neck. "I'm not going to lie, I do want you for sex. A lot of fucking sex." His tongue painted a line along the seam of her lips. "But I want everything. Your body, your mind. Everything."

"Why did you warn me about having sex with you then?"

His jaw clenched. "I'm not doing any of this lightly. No one gets in my life. Ever. Once I let you in, you're mine. I own you, and there's no going back."

Her pussy flooded with warmth. She should hate those words. Her entire life was devoted to her independence and personal power. But Shadow didn't want to hurt her. He wanted her as his woman, and nothing could have been more flattering to her. The feeling of being chosen was new and addictive. She didn't realize how desperately she needed his reassurance, confirmation he wouldn't walk away like all the others.

"What about you? Will you be mine, or do you get to run around on me?"

Shadow frowned. "Why would you say that? If you're mine, I'm yours. Ever since that night in your backyard, I knew you were the one, but I fought it." He ran the pad of his thumb along her lower lip. "Tell me you want to be my woman, Riley."

"I like the sound of that."

He kissed her lips, soft and gentle. "I'll never let anyone hurt you."

"That'll take some getting used to. No one's ever stood up for me before."

He stared at her, no humor in his eyes. "If anyone

fucks with you, I'll kill them." His words took her breath away, not just because of the way he said them, but because she knew he was telling her a fact.

"How about we start with that real date you owe me."

He smiled. "This weekend. I promise."

Weekend? The sudden realization hit her hard. "The bakery! I forgot to set my alarm." She glanced at her night-side clock. It was almost eight in the morning, and she should have been baking hours ago. Riley jumped out of bed and raced to the bathroom.

Riley poked her head back in the bedroom a while later, a toothbrush in her mouth. She was going to tell Shadow he could stay in bed and let himself out, but he was already dressed and checking his cell phone.

"I'll drive you to work," he said.

She shook her head. "You don't have to do that. Besides, I have some supplies I need to bring in the trunk of my car." Should she ask about his day? Something along the lines of, *who are you going to kill today?* She was never going to get used to dating a hitman.

Once they were finally outside, she pushed her purse up higher on her shoulder, and locked the front door. As soon as she turned around, Shadow pressed her against the door, no space between them. He cupped her face and kissed her hard on the mouth. She felt his hard cock against her stomach, and she wished she had another hour of time to spend with him. In fact, she was tempted to let him take her right there on the front stoop.

"The neighbors will talk," she said against his lips.

"Let them talk. I don't care what the neighbors think." He reached down and cupped her ass. "I want you in my bed tonight, Riley Church."

Her words came out breathless. "Your house?"

She'd never seen inside his house besides the times she'd peeked in his windows. It felt like being invited to his private, forbidden lair.

He nodded, and gave her a final kiss. "Call me if you need me."

Riley sat in her car and watched Shadow walk over to his garage, the door rising up automatically. A minute later, his black SUV backed out, the windows too heavily tinted for her to see his face. And then he disappeared up the street. Her curious mind wondered where he was going. Was he off to kill that man from the restaurant? Would he even come home in one piece?

****

Shadow had left Riley's house in the middle of the night for a couple hours. He had to crack the cell phone and dig up intel on his mark. He'd taken a cold shower and loaded up his truck with his arsenal before returning to Riley's bed. Everything was ready to go. Now that he had a location, the job was as good as done.

He hit the highway. There was a boat coming in the old harbor in an hour. Thanks to Riley, he had all the information he needed. His mark was meeting with a buyer and then a new plastic surgeon. In their underground world, there was a network of medical professionals willing to do just about anything off the books. Shadow's mind was focused on the task at hand, but that girl still played in the back of his head.

My girl.

He'd spent his life in a numb state, refusing to get close to anyone. After his mother, the man who'd mentored him and introduced him to Boss had also died of cancer. At that point, Shadow decided it was better never to get emotionally involved with anyone. He'd lived alone, focused on work, and put on a mask that hid the pain. Now he'd transformed into some lovesick schoolboy, unable to think about anything but one woman.

He called Killian as he drove. "Hey, how are things settling out for you?" Since they'd been on assignment together, taking down part of the Dead Angels MC, they hadn't spoken. Killian had reunited with the mother of his son, and they were supposed to be starting fresh. Shadow wanted the best for them, even though family life wasn't in the cards for him.

"We bought a house on the water, about ten minutes from Viper." Killian laughed out loud. "Can you believe that shit?"

"The kid getting on okay?'

"Yeah, we have Killian Junior enrolled in school, and I'm keeping on top of him. So far, so good. I can't complain."

"That's great. I'm glad things are working out. You deserve it."

There was a brief silence on the line. "Hey, I know you didn't call to shoot the shit, Shadow. What's up?"

He gritted his teeth, not knowing where to start. "How's Boss handling your new family? He okay with June, or do you think he'll make trouble?"

"I'm still working for Killer of Kings, watching his back, so he can't complain."

"You're not worried about your woman?"

"Boss might be a hard ass, but I know he's happy for me in his own way. For Viper and Bain, too. Finding a good woman in our line of work is like winning the fucking lotto. You hope for it, but never expect it to happen."

Talking about his personal life felt foreign, and if he hadn't felt comfortable with Killian, he never would have asked for his advice. "I've been dating this girl,"

Shadow started. "Of course, Boss found out about it. He said I could find happiness with a woman like her, same as you."

"What's wrong with that?"

"I don't trust him, not a fucking word. I feel like he's setting me up, going to use her against me. I know he gets a hard-on having leverage over everyone."

Killian exhaled. "You love her?"

Shadow licked his lips. What the fuck was love? "I don't know."

"Then can I have a go with her?"

Shadow silenced, his body tensing up ... just as Killian started laughing on the other end.

"You're whipped, bud. You love her or Boss wouldn't have mentioned anything. When was the last time he tried to fix you up with a whore?"

"I don't know if I can do it, the whole relationship thing. My life's too dangerous. I'd never forgive myself if something happened to her because of me."

"Fuck that shit, Shadow. If you love her, claim her, keep her safe. It's what we've been fucking trained to do, eh?"

"Thanks," he said. "Hey, take care of that kid. If he's anything like you, he's a pain in the ass."

Killian chuckled before hanging up.

The pier was just ahead. Shadow pushed away his thoughts of Riley and focused on his mission. A distraction could get him killed.

He parked in a nearby alleyway and made his way on foot after strapping his body with heat. Shadow moved without a sound, blending into the surroundings invisibly. The large wooden crates and metal containers near the docks gave him plenty of vantage points. When he saw Chains hiding behind one of the large crates, his hackles went up. What the fuck was Chains doing there? How could he know the mark would be at the dock? Even Shadow wouldn't have known without that cell phone, but then again, Chains had been at the restaurant. Shadow didn't know if he was with Killer of Kings or the damned enemy.

He moved in, twisting a silencer onto the muzzle of his Glock. When he was right behind the asshole, he pressed the gun to Chains's head. "Funny to find you here," he said.

Chains put both his hands up at his sides. "It's not what you think."

"If I were you, I'd start explaining real fast."

He didn't stop Chains as he slowly turned around. "You know Boss has eyes and ears everywhere. I'm only supposed to keep tab, but this hit is all you, Shadow. Actually, the real reason I'm here is because of him."

Shadow narrowed his eyes and looked to where Chains pointed. In the distance, he saw a figure lying prone position with a sniper rifle. "Who the hell is that?"

"It's a big contract. You have to know Killer of Kings isn't the only one looking to cash in on it," said Chains. "This guy's the only one Boss is worried about."

Shadow lowered his weapon. "You have anything on him?"

"He's bad news. Colombian. Rumor has it his parents sold him to one of the big barrio gangs when he was just a kid. By the time he was a teen, he took out the leader and brought the gang to the next level."

"So he's got killing in his blood."

"When he was in his twenties, the kingpin of the largest drug cartel sought him out, wanted to hire him for protection. Long story short, he gained the kingpin's trust, then cut out his heart. He's a savage bastard."

"And he wants my paycheck. That doesn't sit well with me."

"They call him El Diablo," said Chains.

"Boss want you to take him out?"

Chains shook his head. "That's a last resort. Boss wants me to recruit him."

"Shit," said Shadow. "That would be a problem for me."

"Just worry about your contract. I'll keep him busy."

Shadow adjusted his harness, and checked the clip in his Glock. "If he gets in my way, I *will* kill him."

"Fair enough."

He moved in closer, slipping in and out of the paths between containers, unseen as he neared the location. His mark from the restaurant stood in between his men, adjusting the collar of his jacket. That smug prick thought he was invincible, but he never expected Killer of Kings.

Never expected Shadow.

He pulled out the sniper rifle he had strapped to his back, bent down on one knee and adjusted his sights, taking his time. This was what he lived for, what he was trained to do. He took out his target with one clean shot. A rush ran though his body, making his cock hard, when the mark collapsed to the ground. Shadow dropped the rifle and stood up, shooting the scrambling men one by one until only the caw of seagulls and waves slashing the dock filled the air.

He took a deep breath of the salty air, and noticed El Diablo packing up from his distant position on the metal container.

His intuition nagged him to check up on Riley. That asshole and his entourage had seen her last night. Shadow hated entangling Riley into his world, but all he could do now was work hard to keep her safe. He pulled out his cell phone and logged into the security system he set up in the bakery. There were a few customers in the store, settling his nerves slightly. He zoomed in when he saw a man looking through a cake book with Riley, his hand on her shoulder. That's when he saw it.

The tattoo.

The infinity symbol Maurice had shown him.

Thanks to Riley's lip reading, he knew his mark was on to him, so all the doubles probably had the tattoo by now. Shadow felt lightheaded, his heart hammering in his chest. That same feeling of helplessness he'd known too well as a child, infused into his blood. It was a twenty-minute drive back to the plaza. The mark was dead, but he must have already sent a hit out on Riley. One of his fucking body doubles was at the bakery.

He called Riley as he rushed back to his car. She didn't answer. *Shit!*

Shadow sped down the side streets to get to the highway. His only mission was getting to his woman. Everything else could wait. As he drove, his cell rang. He used his hands-free system as he wove in and out of traffic.

"I see your intel panned out," said Boss. "Good work."

"Not now. There's a hitman at the bakery. Why the fuck didn't you have Chains bury these fuckers weeks ago?"

"Killer of Kings runs like a choreographed dance. It's a thing of beauty," said Boss, his voice carrying the usual calming timbre. "And for God's sake, Shadow, we're not primitive. Everyone working for me has a unique skillset, far beyond these so-called hitmen for hire. Sometimes I like to challenge my men, sometimes I teach them lessons."

"Look, I get it, but this isn't a fucking game! Riley's life is in danger." He remembered how Boss had taught Killian a lesson about killing women. Shadow wasn't some new recruit. He'd been killing all his life, and besides a few hiccups, he did his job well.

"How far will you go to save her, Shadow?"

Chapter Eight

This guy didn't want to book or arrange a cake. Riley played along though. She didn't exactly have much choice. When the guy put his hand on her shoulder, she wanted to vomit, but again, like every other time she was faced with a hard decision, she kept her cool.

Tucking her hair behind her ear, she saw several girls enter the shop.

"You keep looking while I serve." She smiled up at him, and went behind the counter to serve the young girls. She didn't alert them to the fact there was a monster in their midst. They didn't need to know that kind of shit.

The man in question was staring at her, and she didn't really have time to get Shadow on the phone. This was one of the men from the restaurant. She didn't like this one bit. Why would this guy suddenly want anything to do with her? It was a set-up. Growing up on the streets, in between foster homes, she'd come to realize at a young age when danger lurked.

Releasing a breath, she looked around, and saw that no one was around.

"So, have you picked a design yet?" she asked, moving toward him.

"I was wondering if you could show me some of the cake sizes. I'm sorry, I really don't get the whole size and look ratio thing. All of these cakes look really small, and I won't do small."

You're a fucking liar.

If he got her to go to the back of the bakery, he was going to try to kill her. Avoiding the bakery would arouse his suspicions and right now, she just wanted to live through the next few minutes.

If I live through this I swear I'm going to stop stressing about the little things, and enjoy life. I'll have sex more. I'll do more of everything and less of the boring stuff. I'll live my life to the fullest and never allow a dull moment to interrupt my awesomeness.

She thought about Shadow and how he'd made her feel in the few times they'd been together. Last night had been magical, and the thought of never seeing him again, filled her with pain.

"Sure. Two seconds. Let me just lock the door so no one comes in and tries to steal the stuff that I've got on offer." Her heart raced as she flicked the lock into place. *I can do this.*

Smiling at the man, she walked into the back of her bakery.

He was close behind her, and within seconds he had a gun pressed against her skull. Reaching into her pocket, she felt the only thing that she knew how to use. Breathing in and out, she closed her eyes.

"You really shouldn't have fallen into my lap so easily." He spun her around, and she forced herself to look at him. To stare at the man who intended to kill her. "It's a shame. You're pretty for a fat girl. I'd have loved to fuck you, but I don't have time. I've got to meet my boss. I can't keep him waiting." His gaze ran down her body, but she didn't think. She stomped on his foot, and jarred her elbow into his stomach.

The shock of her attack put him in a vulnerable position, and after he'd pressed a gun to her temple, she wasn't in a forgiving mood. She was pissed off. Without another thought to what she was doing, she plunged the blade into the bastard's eye, pulling it out, and stabbing him in the throat. She acted on pure adrenaline, her only thought to survive, and she took the guy by surprise.

She gasped, and stepped away, holding the knife in her hand like it was a lifeline. The man gargled, screamed, and then fell to the floor, blood dripping from his eye and his neck. She had just killed a man, and she stared down at the floor where he'd collapsed into a heap, frozen in place.

"Well, I have to say I'm surprised."

Riley spun around and saw Boss standing in the entryway. "But I locked the door."

"Being the owner of Killer of Kings, you learn a few things. Like getting spare keys to the places of the women in your workers' lives. Shadow has been interested in you for some time. I thought he'd have actually taken you by now, but he was always a bit of a dramatic bastard, and self-serving as well. The martyr."

She pointed at the man on the floor. "He was going to kill me."

"Yes. I don't think he anticipated the knife, do you?" He laughed. "The name's Boss, by the way." He held his hand out for her, and she merely stared at it.

"Are you high?" Her hand was covered in blood, and she'd killed a man. All of the evidence was in her bakery, and she had nothing to tell the cops, and her life had just gone to shit. Everything was collapsing on her.

Suddenly Boss caught her arms, holding her up. "Don't freak out on me."

"I'm really kind of losing it right now. I don't need to be dealing with this."

"Take a deep breath."

"Get your hands off her," Shadow said, appearing behind Boss. "How the hell did you get here before me?"

Two other big men entered the bakery soon after Shadow. She still held the knife in her hand and she stared at Shadow, needing him more than anything, but Boss didn't let her go.

"Apparently, she had it all under control." Boss finally released her, and she began to shake. Boss leaned down, and checked the tattoo. He whistled. "Another body double. Shit, there'll be a lot of these fuckers out of work now."

"What the fuck is the meaning of this?" A guy with an accent spoke up, and she frowned. "That was supposed to be my mark."

"You didn't get the hit, El Diablo, Shadow did. I never doubted him." Boss grabbed the knife from her hand, closing it up, and pocketing it. That was the knife that had gotten her through many scrapes and there was no way in hell that anyone was going to take that away from her.

"Give me back my knife." Whatever shock or trance she'd been in faded at him stealing her knife.

Boss ignored her and faced the other men. He began to talk, but she wasn't listening to him. Her mind buzzed, and she felt faint, but she was still determined to get what belonged to her.

"Give me back my damn knife." Her temper began to increase, and she really, really needed her knife back. Her sanity slowly slipped away. When he didn't give it to her, she took matters into her own hands, and shoved her hand in his pocket.

Boss caught her hand, holding her wrist, and applying a great deal of pressure. Before she realized what was happening, guns were pointed at all of them.

"I just want my knife back," she whispered, her fire dwindling.

"It's covered with blood," Boss said. "You were clearly having a hard time dealing with it."

"It's not the first time it's been covered with blood." She stared at Boss. "Give it back. Please."

He sighed, pulling the blade out of his pocket, placing it in her hands. She wrapped her fingers around it, ignoring the men as she went to her sink. All of the food she had was going to have to be tossed out. Everything.

She couldn't afford this kind of loss, not right now.

"Are you okay?" Shadow asked, coming toward her.

She glanced up at him, seeing the concern on his face.

"I'm fine." Right now, she didn't want to talk.

"We'll take care of everything. A cleaning crew will be here and you won't have to see any of it."

Riley snorted. "I'll be seeing this stuff in my nightmares tonight." She cleaned the blade and winced as she cut herself. Her hands were shaking, and no matter what she did, she couldn't get them to stop. Gritting her teeth, she dropped the blade into the sink, and Shadow took over. He grabbed her wrists, and tutted. He pulled her into the small bathroom, closing the door, hiding them away.

He cupped her face, tilting her head back. "I had no idea that asshole was coming here."

"You were going to hit him, right?"

"I was going to do more than hit him, I was going to fucking kill him."

"I saved you a job."

"Yeah, and Boss is thinking of paying you."

She tilted her head to the side. "What kind of money are we talking about here?"

"The kind of money that will stop you worrying for a while. You'd be able to invest in a new kitchen with all the latest gadgets."

Riley smiled. "That would be nice. To not have to worry about money. Does Boss have a job opening?"

Shadow shook his head. "No, this life is not for you, and I won't let you try this shit either. It's dangerous, scary, and you don't need to deal. You're a baker. Not a killer."

"I'm starting to think I should pick another

profession." She stared down at her hands, which were soaked with blood. Hers and that of the man that was going to kill her. Biting her lip, she felt tears spring to her eyes, and she moaned. "I killed someone today."

"I know, baby."

"He had a gun pressed against my head, and I realized I didn't want to die."

"You did the right thing. That man didn't deserve to live, and he sure as hell didn't deserve to take you from me." He pressed a kiss against her lip. "You didn't do a bad thing."

"I killed a man. In no way is that normal. That is crazy and insane, and that makes me a monster."

She began to hyperventilate.

This was all just too much. Between discovering that Shadow was a hitman, and that a murderer had tried to kill her, she couldn't think.

"Baby, look at me."

She hugged her chest, and she was trying to focus. The door to the bathroom slammed open. Boss and the two other men were there. She was starting to see spots, and everything was spinning.

"You're going to have to shoot her up," Boss said. "She's going to hurt herself."

There was screaming, and Riley was surprised to hear that it was her. She was losing her mind.

"Baby!" Shadow grabbed her, but it was no use. She couldn't stop it. All of the occasions of her past, and everything else, it was just too much. Every single memory, every single pain, it was all there, blooming within her chest, and she couldn't make it stop.

"I'm sorry," Shadow said.

Something pinched her arm, and it wasn't long before the world went blank.

****

Shadow caught Riley in his arms before she completely passed out. He wouldn't let her fall, and he'd never seen a woman lose it so quickly. This wasn't just about the man she'd just killed. He'd seen the horror in her eyes, and in that one action, all of the pain from her past had come through, trapping her. Lifting her up in his arms, he looked at Boss.

"Women really don't know when to shut up," Boss said.

"This shouldn't have happened."

"I know, but who would have known he'd take a hit out on a girl that stole his phone?" Boss shrugged. "Talk to Killian, Viper, even fucking Bain. Women in this industry are going to get hurt. There's no way you can stop it."

"I don't want her hurt."

"Yeah, well, you're going to have to protect her now."

"What the fuck does that mean?" asked Shadow.

"They know her. She's made herself a target. We'll get this place cleaned up, but she can't come back here until we get everyone available in his little circle," Boss said. He turned to look at El Diablo. "What about you? Are you willing to take a chance with the good guys?"

Shadow rolled his eyes.

"You're not the good guys. No one is a good guy. Killing a man to save someone, still makes you a murderer," El Diablo said, spitting on the floor.

"Yeah, I can do without the philosophy debate. Really not interested. I only care if you can kill and do the job quietly." Boss handed him a card. "There's a price tag for every kill related to that fucker." He turned back to Shadow. "Hide her."

"What do you know?" Shadow asked.

"I know that people like this bastard have a following. She's going to be on their shit list, so be ready to start a mass kill. We're going to need to take them all out." Boss stared at her. "This wasn't her first kill."

Shadow didn't say anything. He'd already figured that out.

"Protect her," Boss said, stepping away.

He didn't wait around to question Boss's sudden protective nature. This was one of those moments where Boss confused him.

Taking her out to the car, he lowered her into the back seat, closing the door. Climbing inside, he took off, knowing there was only one place he could go. The injection he'd given her would have her out cold for a few hours, and he had time to get her settled.

Never had he been more terrified than seeing that fucker in the bakery where she worked. He'd raced to get there, but he'd been too late. He couldn't bring himself to even think of life without her.

Damn it.

How had his neighbor gotten under his skin so fucking fast? He didn't want to even think about it. Pulling up outside of the gym, he picked her up out of the car.

Ronny was outside having a smoke, which he tossed away the moment he saw Shadow.

"I didn't know you were coming."

"What have I told you about that shit? It'll fucking kill you if you keep it up." He nodded for Ronny to open the door, and he did. It wasn't long before several of the guys were surrounding him. "Give me some space."

They stepped back. "That's the chick from the other night," one of the boys said.

"I'm taking her back to the office. None of you

have used it to fuck, have you?"

"No, sir," they all said, making his head spin.

"If I find out you have, I'll punish you all." He stepped around the young men, and took Riley straight to the office.

There wasn't anything out of place. He doubted they'd have broken his rules about using his office. Placing Riley on the sofa, he grabbed a blanket to place over her.

"She OD'd or something?" Ronny asked.

Shadow stroked the hair back from her face. The blood on her hands was still there. He had a small bathroom, and he stood shaking his head. "No, she hasn't. I've given her something to help her sleep."

He filled a small bowl with some soapy water, and a sponge. Picking up the first aid kit on the way out, he sat down beside her, and started to work on the hands, being careful not to damage the cut, which was still bleeding.

Once he had her hands clean, he went about cleaning out the cut. Ronny had left, only to return five minutes later. "I don't know if you want any clean clothes. These have come back from the laundry. They don't have blood on them or anything."

"Thank you," Shadow said.

Ronny came from a really bad life. His stepfather used him as a punching bag until Shadow showed him how to use his fists. All of the boys at the gym needed help, and Shadow had used his spare time to teach them all how to take care of themselves, the same way his mentor had with him. Of course, they were boys to him, but most were in their early twenties, some older teens.

It was his one good deed out of a lifetime of death. Rubbing at his temple, he closed his eyes, thinking about how he could have found Riley dead on the floor.

The image drove him nuts.

"We had no idea this was your chick."

"Don't worry about it, Ronny. What happened, happened. Next time a woman comes into the gym, don't try and scare her away with fear of rape. That shit's not good. It's never good." Riley was a strong woman, but she needed taking care of.

"Sure, sir. It won't ever happen again."

He didn't correct him this time. No matter how many times he told Ronny not to call him sir, the kid always did. "Make sure everyone else knows it as well." He looked toward him. "Will you give me some privacy now?"

"Sure, sure."

Ronny closed the door behind him, and Shadow was left alone with Riley. Pulling back the blanket he began to work her clothes off, taking care as he did. She may be out for the count but that didn't mean she had to be pulled all over the place.

"I was just supposed to have some downtime in between hits. It wasn't supposed to be spent getting to know everyone. All I wanted was the chance to fit in. I earn enough to be locked up in a palace or own an island. I didn't want any of that. Just a nice place to pretend that I was normal, that killing people really didn't bother me. What did I get? I got a nosy neighbor with the most haunted eyes I've ever seen. Not to mention the curviest butt that fits really nice against my dick. Let's see, your tits are more than a handful, and I love holding them. Then of course, your laugh. I crave your laugh so damn much, and I think it's because you don't do it enough. You need to laugh all the time, Riley. Life's too short to go around being miserable. You hear me?" He continued to talk to her as he changed her from the clothes she wore to the gym wear.

Afterward, he needed to clear his head. Leaving his office, he grabbed a coffee from the machine, and watched as a couple of boys practice moves in the ring. So long as they fought cleanly without risk of hurting anyone, he didn't mind.

When he returned to the office, Riley was still out cold. Taking a seat behind his desk, he pulled up the footage at her bakery. He'd installed security for him to watch her every chance he got. Rewinding back to when the bastard had her looking through cakes and designs, he watched her serve a bunch of girls. She started talking with the guy, and then closed the door that locked her away with a murderer rather than running out into the busy plaza.

The cameras changed, and he watched her appear. Her eyes closed as the gun pressed against her temple. Death clearly in her sights. How quickly she moved shocked him. Standing on his foot, slamming her elbow against his stomach, and that knife making quick work ending his life. Luckily, he was a low-ranking newbie compared to some of the mark's other men.

Riley's actions were from someone used to defending herself.

Glancing over at her sleeping form, he knew from her files that she'd been in foster care, and also that she'd been working the streets for a long time.

The mask he put on for their world to see, she wore every single day as well. Time passed, and he sat, waiting for Riley to wake up, hoping Boss hadn't given him too high of a dose for her.

He got the message from Boss that the bakery was clean, and everything had been replaced. The fucker was going to make sure she got rewarded for her hard work, not that Shadow had a problem with that.

After what felt like a lifetime, but only a few

hours had passed, Riley began to stir. Getting up from his chair, he moved toward her side, taking hold of her hand as she groaned, opening her eyes.

She turned toward him. "What happened?"

He didn't say a word, allowing her to get accustomed to the passing time, and everything else. She rubbed at her eyes, and began to sit up when she realized her clothes were different.

"You're at the gym with me. One of the guys found some clothes that I could give you so that you wouldn't be in the stuff you wore before."

"The ones covered with blood?"

"You remember?" he asked.

"Yes." She glanced around the room. "What's happening? What's going on?"

"Don't stress about it, baby. You don't need to worry, okay?" He placed a hand on her chest, keeping her down. He moved so that he sat on the edge of the sofa, keeping her in place. "Everything has been taken care of."

"My bakery?"

"Is fine. Everything has been scrubbed and cleaned. All of your products replaced. Boss is very thorough. You could eat off the floors."

She nodded her head, and slowly lay back down.

"He also wants to reward you."

"Reward me?"

"You killed that man. You're going to get paid. It will help you."

Riley closed her eyes. "I should be thrown in jail."

For several seconds Shadow didn't say anything. He held her hand, wondering what to say. Kissing her knuckles, he stared into her eyes. "He wasn't the first man you killed, was he?"

Tears filled her eyes as she shook her head. She didn't try to deny it. "No."

"Tell me, Riley."

There was so much she kept bottled up, and he hated seeing her like this.

She closed her eyes, and sighed. "Sixteen. I was sixteen, and finally getting by. I had a, erm, a fake ID. I got to work, and everything was fine. You know? Nothing going wrong. I worked late one night, finishing at two in the morning. I hadn't been to school in a long time, and I passed this same alley for weeks, months even. They say your life can change in an instant. I was pulled into that alley." She wiped under her nose as the tears fell. "I don't even know who the guy was, I just know that he'd been waiting for me. That's what he said. He'd seen me. He'd been waiting, and I struggled. He slammed me up against the wall, and threw me to the ground, knocking the wind right out of me. I fought, but he was stronger. I screamed for help. I yelled and screamed and begged. Nothing. He didn't stop. He shoved up my skirt, and tore at my panties, and he had his … thing out. I don't know what happened next, but I had the knife in my hand, and I just kept stabbing and stabbing until there was so much blood that all I could see was red." She looked toward him.

"Is that why you wouldn't let Boss have the knife?"

She nodded. "It's kept me safe ever since."

Chapter Nine

Riley had nodded on and off, but Shadow let her rest. When she pushed to sit up on the sofa, he bent down in front of her and held her hands in his.

"How you feeling?"

"Better. I'm sorry for making such a scene," she said.

He couldn't help but smile. "You're allowed to be upset, Riley. Do you think the gossipy housewives on our street could handle what you've just been through?"

She chuckled. "I'd pay to see that."

Shadow sat beside her on the sofa, putting his arm around her so she could rest her head on his chest. "Things are only going to get better. My contract's been handled, and I'll be sure to keep future projects far from home."

"So, no more hitmen waiting to kill me?"

He couldn't answer her without lying. Boss's words rang in his head. The mark's outer circle could still want Riley dead. Until he knew exactly what they were dealing with, he had to keep his woman close. "Let's hope not."

She held his hand. "You have a strong heartbeat," she said.

"I take good care of it," he said. "Now that I think of it, most of my life my biggest fear was dying of sickness. All that's changed now."

"How so?" she asked.

"Because none of that matters anymore. Now I'm only afraid of losing you, Riley."

She tilted her head to kiss him, slowly, passionately.

"I've always been scared to rely on another person. Everyone's always let me down, hurt me, or put me last. I promised myself I'd never give anyone power over my heart … until you came along."

He kissed her again, their tongues playing, tender and sweet. It wasn't a prelude to sex, just unadulterated desire and love for one woman. "You've taken care of yourself for so long, but I'm telling you, you don't need to. I'll never let anyone hurt you," he promised.

Once the gym had been closed down at midnight, Shadow drove Riley to his house. Even though he had her little bungalow wired from top to bottom, it didn't have the security measures he had in place. There was no way he'd leave her in harm's way now that she was on a massive shit list.

They'd stayed at the gym until late in the evening, had some takeout, and did a lot of talking. Now it was time to get down to business, but first he wanted Riley safe and settled so she could rest.

"I know you wanted a sleepover at your place tonight, but I didn't think it would be under these circumstances," said Riley, as they walked up the path to his front door.

No one had ever been in his home besides Boss. No women. No colleagues.

"It's the best place to be for now," he said. "Until I figure things out, I don't want you alone. Or at your bakery."

Once inside the foyer, she kicked off her shoes, still a little wobbly, so he held her elbow. "I can't ignore my bakery. I'll lose all my customers," she said absently, busy looking around.

"If you want a replay of today, be my guest, but it may not turn out as well for you next time."

"I can't believe this is happening. It's like the witness protection program, only I'm on my own."

Shadow tilted her chin up. "You're not alone. You

have me. I won't let anything happen to you. If they come, and they will, I'll take care of them."

"Aren't you scared?"

He smiled. "I was only afraid when I couldn't get to you in time, when I thought that asshole had killed you. I felt helpless, and I won't be so sloppy next time."

"It wasn't your fault. You couldn't have known."

Shadow didn't want to get Riley upset or to revisit memory lane again, so he thought it best to change the subject. "Do you need to talk more?" The drugs had worn off hours ago, and the food helped stave off the lingering effects.

"I feel like an emotional basket case, but other than that, I'll live. It was a moment of weakness, but I'm good now."

"You don't have to be strong all the time. It's not healthy," he said.

"You should take your own advice. How do you deal with your shitty past?"

"I joined the Marine Corps, did my time—it only made things worse. It fucked with my head to the point they wouldn't let me return after my third tour."

"But you're still killing."

"That's different. I don't mind the violence. I appreciate the outlet," he said. "The gym helps, too."

He pointed to the living room, inviting her to have a seat.

She shook her head. "I've seen this room. I want to see the rest of your house," she said.

"Right, you've peeked in most of my windows, haven't you?"

Riley shrugged. "You wouldn't talk to me, so I had no choice. I don't like mysteries I can't solve."

"Okay, go at it."

She pushed open the door off the main living

room, stopping dead in her tracks. "Holy shit!"

Shadow chuckled as he past her, pulling the handgun out of his waistband and dropping it on the counter.

"I thought this would be the kitchen." She stood in awe as she looked around his vault, the secure room housing his weapons and ammo. He'd been collecting for a long time.

"No way did I expect this, and I imagined a lot of scenarios." Riley ran her fingertips along the shelving, checking out everything as if doing inventory. "Do you even have a kitchen?"

"It's in the back of the house," he said. "Look, I don't like leaving you alone right now, but I need to meet with Killer of Kings and find out where we stand."

"I can handle myself. I'm a big girl." Riley smiled, mischief in her eyes. "Besides, I'll be busy exploring for a while."

"Leave me a shred of privacy, please." He cupped her face, kissing her softly on the lips. "Don't leave the house, baby. Take a shower, get some sleep. I'll be back before you wake up."

Before Shadow left the house, he turned on the exterior security system. If Riley sensed anything suspicious, he told her to call his cell right away. Chains was waiting for him in an abandoned parking lot half an hour away. Shadow was made of questions, and demanded answers.

When he arrived on location, he backed into a parking spot, maintaining a good view of the area. The distant street lights gave a faint glow to the dark parking lot. When he saw the interior lights of a car flick on, he got out of his truck, palming the weapons under his jacket.

"Can you explain what the fuck happened today?"

he asked as he approached.

Chains cracked his neck to each side, leaning against the hood of his car. "None of us knew that shit was on to her." The passenger side of the car opened, and El Diablo stepped out.

"What the fuck is he doing here?"

Chains put up a hand to stop Shadow from pulling out his Glock. "When El Diablo saw you take off, he followed. The contract was worth a shitload of money, and he thought you had another lead. My job was to tail him."

Shadow had wondered why the fuck Chains and El Diablo were on his ass when he arrived at the bakery, but he'd only had Riley on his mind at the time. If they'd gotten in his way, he wouldn't have hesitated to take them both out.

"Well the mark is dead, so only I'll be getting paid."

El Diablo ran a hand through his black hair. He had an elaborate tattoo on the right side of his face near his eye. The bastard hadn't said a word.

"What's he doing here? Boss hire him?"

"I don't work for anyone," said El Diablo. "But I came this far, so I don't want to leave empty handed."

"You're far from home. It's a long flight back to Colombia," said Shadow.

El Diablo narrowed his eyes, his body mostly covered in darkness. "I haven't been back there in over ten years. This is where I play now."

"Great. Just what we need, another psychopath loose on the streets."

"Watch it, gringo."

Shadow was fluent in Spanish among several other languages. And this asshole didn't intimidate him. "Do you expect us to call you El Diablo? Give us a real name or I'll have to make one up. How about Fred?"

"Fuck off."

Chains exhaled. "Let's *not* do this right now. All I want is hard liquor and pussy. I didn't sign on to play babysitter to you two fuckers."

"Boss said something about the mark's inner circle looking for revenge. Do we have numbers? How much do they know?"

"They'll be going after the girl again. She has ties to Killer of Kings, and they have her pic and info from the brush at the restaurant."

"How?"

"He wasn't worth a fortune for nothing. As soon as his phone went missing, he had his men pull the security camera footage in the restaurant."

"Well, he's pushing daisies, so what are we dealing with?"

"Boss wants things cleaned up. There's a pretty penny for every kill loyal to the mark. There're at least a dozen that we know of."

"That's why I'm here." El Diablo winked. "I need to clean up your mess."

"Listen, Fred, I wasn't asking you."

"Do you hear this asshole?" El Diablo asked Chains. "Tell him how many men I've killed."

"Let's not start a fucking pissing contest, ladies." Chains scrubbed his hands over his face. "Just call him Xavier. It's his given name."

"Motherfucker." Xavier whirled around, a handgun outstretched in his hand. "Why'd you tell him my name?"

"I'm not crazy about calling you El Diablo either. Save it for someone who gives a shit," said Chains. "Now, Boss is sending us encrypted files, so check your emails. Shadow, keep your woman on a tight leash.

They'll be looking for her, and they won't ask questions first."

"They should be after me, not her. I'm the one who killed their boss. I don't want her in danger."

"Too late for that, big boy." Chains opened the driver's side door. "We'll all be sleeping with one eye open until this shit's cleaned up."

Shadow watched as the car drove off, leaving him alone in the darkness. He wanted to end this, but couldn't do it on his own. There was a network that needed to be exposed—one by one. He planned to get things started tonight, knocking a couple threats off their list. He knew where two of the mark's bodyguards were staying from his previous intel. Since he was no longer required to play nice and keep his distance, it was time to pay a visit.

He broke into the secure lobby, pistol whipped the lobby guard, and rode the elevator up to their suite on the twenty-second floor. As he walked down the long, quiet hallway, he attached a silencer to his handgun. The shotgun over his shoulder was a last resort.

When he arrived at the room, he heard activity inside, despite the late hour. He prepared himself, picked the lock, then burst into the suite. He aimed at the first man attempting to get out of his chair, shooting him in the chest. As he moved in closer, he added another bullet to the man's head as he continued to scan the suite. After a clean sweep, he kicked open the bedroom door. Two naked whores screamed, struggling to get off the bed. The asshole tried to reach for a gun on the bedside table. Shadow shook his head.

"I need names."

"You'll kill me anyway, so fuck you."

"Wrong answer." Shadow shot him between the eyes, a spray of blood coloring the white sheets. He holstered his weapon and rummaged through the drawers for something he could use. It would have been a waste of time to interrogate the shit.

When he stood back up, one of the women cried out. "Please, we'll do anything…"

He briefly glanced in their direction. "Not interested."

As Shadow drove back home, he punched the dashboard, shaking out his fist afterward. He'd worked so hard to keep his home life and work separate. Just when it looked like he'd get a chance at a real life with Riley, the worlds became blurred. Now he had to worry about assassins showing up on his street or at Riley's bakery. It was bullshit, and seemed he just couldn't get a break in his fucked-up life.

The closer he got to his neighborhood, the more at ease he felt because he was closer to *her*. All he could think about was fucking her, claiming her again and again. He needed her. Tonight, he'd keep his hands to himself, no matter how difficult. The poor little thing been through a lot and needed to rest her body and mind. He wanted to make things better for her—and he would.

****

The first night Riley arrived at Shadow's, she'd showered—the longest shower she'd ever had. It was a symbolic cleansing, allowing all the blood and death and fear to go down the drain. She thought she'd moved on from the nightmares of her past, but it all came rushing back to the surface as soon as she was forced to use her blade again.

That was four days ago.

Riley prided herself on being resilient. She'd had to be all her life. After a day or two she was level headed and felt in charge of her emotions once again. But Shadow continued to keep his distance. At first, she appreciated the fact, knowing he'd put his needs aside for her wellbeing. But four days, *four days*, of watching him walk around in just his jogging pants was a cruel and unusual punishment. Her body was ripe and wanton, memories of their one night together plaguing her thoughts.

Shadow had pull-up bars set up in his bedroom. She was forced to watch him do sets of pull-ups followed by a long series of push-ups several times a day. All she could think about was sex, and licking those glistening muscles. Why was he still holding back? Was he not attracted to her anymore? Did he judge her for killing that man?

Riley finished showering, only slipping on a pair of red lace panties. She'd had enough of waiting for Shadow to make a move. Her desperation combined with being cooped up for four days straight was driving her crazy. She walked into his bedroom, her breasts swaying as she moved. The cool air made her nipples tighten into firm buds. He glanced up at her from where he lounged on the bed with a stack of files. He'd been obsessed with finding all the people that wanted her dead.

He stared, his tongue wetting his lower lip, but the bastard didn't react. Her confidence took a hit, and she wondered where things were going between them. They'd gotten so close the past few days, sharing intimate details about their lives, and she swore they were soul mates. The emotional intimacy had made her want him even more. She was so confused now.

Riley quickly tugged on her clothes, giving up on seducing Shadow.

"I want to go to my bakery," she said, her words clipped.

"I already told you that's not possible. Not yet."

She frowned. "I just want to stop by and take a quick look. I only remember how it looked that day, and I can't get the images out of my head. I want to see it without blood and a dead body on the floor."

"I don't know."

"Listen, I haven't left your house in days. I need fresh air. You'll be with me, so I'll be safe … right?"

He sat up on the edge of the bed. "If we're going to go, it's best to go now before it gets late. It'll have to be quick."

Riley nodded, surprised she'd gotten him to agree so quickly.

Before they left the house, Shadow strapped his body with weapons. Her pussy ached watching his hard body shift, his attention focused. He was danger personified, a skilled killer—and it made her hotter than hell. Unfortunately, she couldn't even give herself away for free. His sweet words and cold actions didn't mesh.

They drove in silence, tension thick in the air. She wished things were the way they used to be. She missed baking, missed not being independent. She missed Shadow's affection most of all. They stopped at a pharmacy and then headed to the plaza.

He parked in front of the bakery. At least it was in one piece, and no broken windows. Shadow came around to her side of the car and opened the door, helping her out. He held her hand as they walked to the entrance. Shadow was on edge, continually scanning the area.

Once inside, he locked the door and pulled down the sun shades.

"Okay, make it quick."

He stood near the entrance as she wandered around, checking for damage and cleanliness. Everything looked in order. In fact, it was a hell of a lot cleaner than she left it. Boss really was thorough. Riley expected to feel a repeat of that traumatic day, but it was gone. She just wanted to move on.

"Shadow?"

He was by her side within seconds. "What's wrong?"

"Nothing. Well, nothing's wrong here. There's obviously something wrong with *us*."

He leaned back, both hands resting on the edge of the counter. "What do you mean?"

"Maybe I'm wrong, but I thought you wanted me to be your woman. Has something changed?" She didn't want to be played, to be just another number to him. It would break her heart. She'd let him in, and allowed herself to fall in love.

"You *are* my woman."

She exhaled, the weight of the world slipping off her shoulders. "Then I don't understand why you've been avoiding me. Are you not attracted to me?"

The corners of his eyes crinkled. "What are you talking about, baby?"

"You. Me. You realize you haven't even kissed me in days. I feel like you can't stand the sight of me." There. She'd put it all out there. He either wasn't attracted to her or had the willpower of a god.

He hooked his fingers around the side of her waist, pulling her close. "You've been through a lot, way too much. I didn't want to push you. I care more about you than sex."

She smiled. "That's good to hear, Shadow, but I promise I'm over it."

"I know you're just trying to be strong."

"No, I'm tired of being rejected by you. The other stuff I can handle, but feeling like my love is one-sided is another thing."

"Love? I thought Riley Church didn't do love." He cupped her cheek, caressing her with his thumb.

"You're impossible," she said.

His scruff was growing in, his eyes tired but hungry. He'd been holding back, she could see that now, and she loved him even more because of fit.

"Do you want me to kiss you?" he asked.

"I want a hell of a lot more than a kiss, but only if you want to. I'm tired of being tolerated by men."

He scoffed. "Tolerated? You've been driving me crazy, teasing every chance you get. You make it hard to be a gentleman."

"So you are attracted to me?"

"My cock's been stiff all week. I thought I'd lose it this morning when you came in the room with no shirt on. I was seconds away from ripping those panties off you."

Her pussy became slick, the rhythmic throb almost unbearable. She squeezed her thighs together in a poor attempt to relieve the ache. "I need you, Shadow," she whispered.

"I'm here, baby. Tell me what you want." He tugged her flush to his body, his erection proof he wasn't lying to her.

"I want you to love me."

"Already done."

"Then, I want you to fuck me."

"Are you sure about that? I've been pent up all week, so I may be a bit rough." He slid his hand past the waistband of her pants, squeezing her ass.

"Right now, I could use a lot of that." She closed her eyes as he nuzzled her neck. His hands were everywhere. She savored his touch, the one she'd been craving all week.

"Take off your clothes, Riley. I want you naked."

He leaned away, waiting for her to comply. "Someone could peek in the windows," she said, taking his hand. She led him to the tiny room she affectionately called her staff room. It was where she took a break or nap, and only consisted of an old tweed sofa and an end table.

Shadow's presence seemed too big in the room, the scent of his masculine cologne intoxicating. She began to strip, too eager to have his body pressed to hers, skin to skin. The first time they'd had sex, it was dark out and happened fast. It had been unexpected, unlike today. She wanted this, demanded this, and with the light of day, there were no secrets.

Once she unfastened her bra, his jaw twitched.

"Keep going, baby girl." He briefly ran his hands over the hard, diagonal bulge in his dark jeans.

She slipped out of her pants and, this time, tossed the red undies.

He hadn't moved, hadn't spoken.

Riley had a lot of curves, and she worried about Shadow's impression of her figure. She felt awkward standing only a few feet from him, completely nude. He wore all black, including a jacket concealing a lot of heat.

"I'm going to fuck you so hard. Come here." He used a crooked finger to beckon her closer. Shadow dropped down to one knee, holding her hips. He buried his face in her tits before sucking on her nipple. She cried out, liquid heat escaping between her legs. "I love these big, juicy tits."

"Oh God…"

He cupped her pussy as he alternated his attention between both breasts. His mouth and tongue were magical, his scruff scraping her sensitive skin. "You're mine, Riley. Only mine. I want to claim every inch of you."

"Yes," she murmured, hardly capable of speech. "Take me, all of me."

He growled as he stood back up. Shadow's

breathing was heavy as he shrugged out of his jacket. She nearly orgasmed when he stood there in just a fitted t-shirt and loaded holsters. His arms were hard, and thick with muscle, the black tattoos reaching his elbows. She wanted to order him to hurry up and fuck her, but kept her mouth shut.

He carefully set both harnesses on the small end table before lifting off his shirt. His chest was chiseled perfection, his abs like a fucking washboard. He reached in his back pocket, pulling out a small box of condoms and tube of lube. He winked and set them down. If he thought she needed added moisture, he was in for a surprise.

"So you were prepared after all," she said, remembering their quick trip to the pharmacy.

"A guy can hope."

She wrapped her fingers around his belt, giving a tug. *He* might have the patience of a saint, but she was running on short supply.

He kissed her, first soft and tentative, then crushing and demanding. He moved forward until she dropped down on the sofa. Shadow braced himself over her, continuing to kiss her lips. The passion between them was off the charts, like two lovers finding each other after a lifetime apart. She couldn't get enough of him.

When he leaned back up, one knee resting on the edge of the sofa, he spread her knees wide. "So fucking pretty," he said. He painted a line with his finger from her navel down to her clit. Her entire body trembled, jolting when he slid two fingers into her cunt. She bucked up to capture more of his fingers. He smiled wickedly. "Patience, baby. Let me play."

"I want your cock," she blurted, beyond caring what she sounded like.

"And you'll get it," he said, his voice silky smooth. "It's all yours." He trailed one of his moistened fingers lower, drawing a circle around her tight asshole. "What about here, Riley? Has a man taken you here?"

She shook her head. Riley was surprised how good it felt to be touched in such a naughty area, like the tickle of a feather. Her sex life didn't consist of anything kinky. In fact, Shadow had opened up a whole new world to her that she was eager to explore. She loved his confidence and ability to take control of any situation. And she trusted him not to hurt her.

"Don't move." He got up and left the room. She could see from the opened door that he was rooting around her baking station. He came back with one of her smooth rolling pins, one she used for small tarts. "What's this?"

"A rolling pin." It was a simple acrylic rolling pin, not the old-fashioned kind he probably expected, made of wood with fancy big handles.

He shrugged. "It'll do. I'll buy you another for the bakery. This one's going to get very dirty."

She watched in rapt fascination as he drizzled some of the lube he bought on the smooth, rounded end. In all the years she'd been baking, she never saw her supplies as sex toys. She felt filthy and wanton, eager for more of Shadow's games.

"Hold your legs open for me, nice and wide." He sat on the end of the couch, leaning over to kiss her clit. She gasped, sinking into the sofa, desperate for more. "You like that?"

"Yes, please don't stop."

He bent over again, lapping at her pussy, teasing and tasting. His rough stubble scraped her sensitive skin, the mix of pain and pleasure driving her wild. The sounds he made were feral, a man barely holding onto his humanity. He assaulted her with his talented mouth, bringing her close but never letting her leap off the edge.

"Watch this, baby." He sat up and replaced his mouth with the lubed rolling pin, swirling it around her entrance. She braced herself up on her elbows to get a full view. He began to push in—slowly, methodically. It began to fill her, disappearing as it entered her cunt. "Oh yeah. So fucking beautiful."

Shadow fucked her with the rolling pin in a slow, teasing rhythm. He used the thumb of his free hand to tease her throbbing clit.

"I'm going to come," she said.

"Good girl. Let me see you come all over this toy. Get it nice and dirty, baby." He moved his thumb in distracting circles, bringing her higher and higher. She grabbed the sofa with both hands as her orgasm railroaded to the surface, forcing her to buck and cry out as waves of pleasure rushed through her.

When she finally settled, opening her eyes, Shadow was unfastening his belt. He kicked off his pants, his cock nearly tearing through his boxer briefs. When he released his erection, she stared, her mouth salivating. The man was hung like a horse, far more impressive than the rolling pin or any man she'd ever dated. He'd be able to fill her to overflowing, and the mere thought nearly made her come again.

"I want your ass, Riley. I want to fill you so full of my cock, I'll be branded on you for life." He grabbed one of the throw pillows and tucked it under her ass, lifting her up higher. He groaned as he slipped a condom over his massive cock, then slathered it with lube. "Such a tight little asshole. You'll feel amazing squeezing my dick. Do you want this, baby?" Shadow slipped a lubed finger into her nether hole, a firestorm of new sensation sparking to life. She was anxious and excited to try this

new forbidden pleasure.
"Yes, give it to me."

Chapter Ten

Never had Riley felt anything so damn intense in her life. Shadow flipped her over and spread the cheeks of her ass apart. She glanced over her shoulder as he once again got her settled on the sofa. He put her hands over her head, pushing her down so that her rear was pushed right up in the air.

Her ass already slick from the lube, she closed her eyes as his cock began to seek entrance into her virgin hole.

"Push out for me, baby. I need you to push out like you're trying to force me out."

She did as he asked, and slowly, he pushed past that tight ring of muscle, and began to fill her ass, going a little deeper each time. She didn't know if she could take much more, especially as he was so big, but the pleasure far outweighed any of the discomfort. She gripped the pillow beneath her head, moaning as he spread the cheeks of her ass once again. His hands were not on his cock anymore, and he slowly filled her ass with every single inch of his impressive cock.

Heat flooded her pussy, and she wanted to play with herself, to push into an orgasm that shook them both.

Shadow was the man for her. She didn't have a single doubt in her mind. His hands moved to her hips, and she gasped as he slammed that last inch, filling her ass. They both groaned, and he leaned over her back, kissing the back of her neck. "You've got all of my cock now, baby. Your tight little ass has it all." He didn't move, giving her time to become accustomed to the feel of his dick in her ass. "Do you like it?"

"Yes."

"Good, because I love the feel of your tight ass

wrapped around my dick. The best feeling in the fucking world, and one I know I can get used to."

Slowly, he began to pull out of her ass so that only the tip of his dick was inside her. She whimpered, not wanting him to stop. She loved the feeling of fullness.

Shadow didn't deny her. The grip on her hips tightened as he filled her. His thrusts were slow and shallow, making her beg him for more. He knew how to tease her so that she was desperate.

"You feel so fucking good. So fucking mine." Shadow growled the words against her neck, biting down, and licking over the pulse. "Touch yourself. I want you to come. I want to feel your ass tighten around me."

Reaching between her thighs, she found her pussy, running her fingers over her swollen clit. The first touch had her gasping, especially as Shadow began to increase the thrusts, driving her closer and closer to the edge of pleasure. She couldn't stand the pain, the pleasure—it was all combining within her, and she knew Shadow had created a monster. These new sensations were addictive.

His touch made her hungry for more, and the grip on her hips, she knew would leave fingerprints.

"I knew the moment I saw you that you were going to be a pain in the ass. I knew I was going to struggle to keep my hands off you, but I fought it. Even as your nosy ass kept butting into my business, making me want you even more. You didn't back down. You're a fighter, exactly like me, and I like that. I want a fighter in my bed, baby. I want you."

She came, screaming his name as he drove harder inside her ass. She felt him tense up, gasp, and then his cock pulsed, filling the condom with his cum.

Seconds later he collapsed over her. His arms went around her, and he was kissing her neck and stroking her body. He held her close so she didn't roll off the sofa.

Riley couldn't believe what they'd just done, but it brought an end to a crazy day. Opening her eyes, she stared across the room at the table and for some strange reason, she thought about Shadow's home. More specifically his front room with the fireplace. His home was so normal for a lot of things. It gave the world the illusion that he was, in fact, normal. She'd slept on his sofa and stared at his fireplace for a couple of hours.

"You're thinking about something. I can feel it. And I probably won't like what you're thinking," he said.

She chuckled. "Just thinking about appearances. Your home looks so normal. Nobody would realize how deadly you are."

She'd killed a man, too.

She'd fallen in love with a killer, and now her life would never be the same.

"My life is in danger," she said.

"I promise you that I won't let anything happen to you. I'll take care of you."

She turned her head to look at him, reaching out to stroke his cheek.

His cock still filled her ass, but she didn't want to move, not for some time.

"It's strange to think of someone taking care of me."

"You better get used to it because I'm not going anywhere." He kissed her palm. "Besides, I own every single part of you now. I've got a few more plans for your body, and you're not going to deny me."

She giggled as he bent down, taking her nipple into his mouth, and biting down to the point of pain that only made her gasp.

"So what happens now?" she asked.

"Now?"

"I feel like Rapunzel. Do I stay in your highly secured home forever, or do I get to leave?"

"You're not in my home right now. We're having a lot of fun. I never thought a bakery could be so … kinky. I'm wondering what I could do with some of those cookie cutters?" He wriggled his brow, making her laugh.

"That roller will not be used for anything in here again," she said.

"I'll take it home with me. It did the job I needed it to do."

"I don't know if that's gross or not." She laughed.

"Don't worry, I'll clean it."

"Be serious. What happens now? I don't want to stay protected forever, and I don't see this working for us, for either of us. What's going to happen?" she asked.

Shadow sighed. "Couldn't you just pretend to be a normal woman for two minutes and not think about everything else?"

She shook her head. "I'm a practical person, Shadow. I need to know what else is going on so I can understand what the hell to do. It's smart to be prepared."

"We need to make sure your life isn't in danger. I'll protect you. You have my promise to take care of you, to love you."

Every time he told her that he loved her, she fell for him a little more. She couldn't help it. There was something irresistible about a guy who didn't have a problem telling a woman how he felt.

"I don't think I can live with having a bodyguard for the rest of my life."

He kissed her cheek. "It won't be for the rest of your life, baby. Just a couple of days until we kill that bastard's inner circle. When they're gone, you'll be free, and then I'm thinking we should go on a vacation."

"A vacation?" Her interest piqued.

"Yeah. Somewhere with the sun beaming down and an ocean to play in."

She shook her head, wrinkling her nose. "I don't do oceans."

"Why not?"

"Sharks."

"We'll go somewhere where there's no sharks."

"You can't guarantee no sharks, Shadow. They're everywhere, and it's the ocean. I'll sunbathe while you go and do your shark diving."

He burst out laughing. "You're a crazy woman, you know that, right?"

"I've lived this long, and I've got no intention of ever, ever, being shark bait. It's not going to happen." She couldn't help but yawn.

"I think it's time we got you home."

He began to pull out of her ass, and she groaned, feeling a bit sore now.

"I'll run you a bath when we get back to my place. I'll take care of you." He used some tissues to wipe up the lube. He removed the condom, wrapping it in more tissue, and threw it in the trash.

Shadow didn't give her the chance to do anything herself. He took care of her, helping her into her clothes before they left the bakery. Being with Shadow was a life she could certainly get used to.

****

Driving back home, Shadow made sure to constantly check his surroundings. The hit out on Riley was serious shit, and he had no intention of losing the only woman he'd ever loved. There were no cars following him, and nothing looked suspicious, even when he made it home noticed nothing was out of the ordinary, which surprised him.

Even he would have been watching the house of a hit, and yet, nothing seemed to be out of place. Checking up and down the street, he rounded the car, opening Riley's door.

"What is it?" she asked.

"Everything's normal."

"That's good, right?"

Shadow shook his head. "You're an easy target, Riley."

"Thanks for the compliment."

"You got that guy last week out of sheer luck. You've got to admit that," he said, turning to her.

"It wasn't *just* luck, Shadow. Being on the streets, you learn to defend yourself. Some of the foster kids would teach each other moves in case they ever got caught. So it wasn't just luck on my side. I had practice, and I'm glad nothing *really* bad happened."

"I'm not disputing that, but this guy was part of something bigger. They'd want revenge, believe me." Something bugged him about all of this, and it pissed him off.

He always listened to his instincts, and right now they were telling him something wasn't right. Entering his home, he punched in the security code.

"Shadow, you're scaring me."

He didn't stop, knowing that Riley would find this out at some point. Going to the basement, he turned on the computer screens that showed Riley's house.

"Holy shit, you were watching me all this time?" Riley leaned over his shoulder.

"You got a problem with that?" he asked, checking each angle of her rooms, and seeing nothing out of place. Nothing was ransacked. The house was empty.

Leaning back, he tapped his knuckles on the edge of the desk aware of Riley staring at him.

"Something is really bothering you," she said.

"You're not going to give me shit about this?"

"Not right now. I think you need to handle whatever it is you've got going on."

He grabbed his cell phone and dialed Chains's number.

"Yeah," Chains said, answering within a couple of rings.

"Has there been any update?" Shadow asked.

"Nothing. Everything's gone quiet, and there's no sign of any action either. The bakery is clear."

Chains had been watching the bakery since they left it.

Shadow stared at the screen. "Something's not right. I'm calling Boss." He hung up the phone, and began to dial Boss.

"What makes you think they'd come after me in the first place?" Riley asked.

"You took out their man. It's logical to go after the person who made the hit."

Boss wasn't answering his cell phone.

"That doesn't necessarily make any sense," Riley said.

With every passing minute he was getting more and more pissed off. Shadow stared at Riley while scrolling through Maurice's contact info on his cell phone. "What the hell do you mean?"

"You work for this Boss, right? He's the one that pulls the strings?"

"Yeah, so?"

"Well, he's the one that took the contract. What's to say there's not one out for him?"

"No one can take down Killer of Kings. Boss is the one that pulls the strings. We bring people down that are no good." He didn't add that they've been known to also kill innocents as well. Sometimes innocent people had to die in order to protect many more people. His job wasn't always fair, but everything he did, he had a reason for.

"So you're known by a lot of people, right? What happens if you've pushed too far? People are probably tired of losing against your organization. Why not take matters into their own hands, and rid themselves of your boss?"

Shadow didn't like that she made sense. Killer of Kings had a fantastic reputation for getting the job done. Boss only ever employed the best men, and he was the deadliest motherfucker alive.

Pressing Maurice's number, he stared at Riley. "I hope you're wrong."

She wasn't wrong. He knew it in his gut more than he knew anything else. It was the only explanation for why Riley hadn't been hit.

"Shadow, thank God, I've been trying to reach everyone. I had to warn you about Boss. His security codes were accessed, and his main building infiltrated with at least a dozen men, maybe more. He sent me a code black," Maurice said.

"A code black, you're sure?" Shadow asked.

"Yes. I've told Viper and Bain. I don't know what to do. Killer of Kings is only worth anything if Boss is alive."

"Maurice, send me Boss's current address and the codes I'll need to access it."

"That's not protocol. He said that when a code black is initiated, you're to get the hell out of Dodge."

"I'm not going to do that. I'm not a fucking coward, and I sure as hell ain't going to hide away and let Boss die." He couldn't do it. For as big a bastard as Boss was, he was still someone Shadow highly respected. A man who'd helped him up when he was down. "I want all that info within the next few minutes."

He didn't waste time talking. Hanging up the phone, he pocketed it, rushing up the stairs toward his weapons room.

"What are you doing?" she asked, chasing behind him.

"I'm going to go and clean up this mess."

"I'm coming with you." She went to grab a rocket launcher, but he stopped her, holding her arm.

"Are you fucking kidding me?" He had to stop himself from laughing. "No, you're not going to be in the line of fire. This isn't your fight. This is mine, and you don't need to be involved." He cupped her cheek. "I won't be able to focus on helping Boss if I'm worried about you." He pressed his lips against hers. "Please, just this once, do as I ask, and stay safe."

He had some hunting to do, and the only way he'd be able to focus was to know she was safe.

She nodded. "Yes."

Shadow wasn't convinced. Pulling her toward him, he saw the tranquilizer darts right behind her. Distracting her with his kiss, he grabbed one, plunging it into her arm. She gasped, but before she could do or say anything, she fell asleep in his arms.

"I'm sorry, babe. You're all I have, and I won't lose you."

Shadow placed her on floor, securing her wrist to the radiator before grabbing his guns. If he was lucky, she'd be out for the count while he dealt with business.

Chapter Eleven

Shadow sped down the highway in his Mustang Shelby. In all the years he'd worked for Killer of Kings, Boss had always answered his cell phone, day or night. He didn't like this at all. A light drizzle rained down on the darkened streets, distorting his view through the windshield.

He'd had a lot of scrapes in his early years as a hitman, and Boss was always ready to bail him out or send backup. He never left his men to fend for themselves, and this was Shadow's chance to show the same loyalty.

His phone rang as he drove. He was so focused, it took a couple rings before he turned on the hands-free. "Yeah."

"Maurice get a hold of you?" It was Bain. He'd only met him on a few brief occasions, and they'd never worked together. He was one of the newest to sign on with Killer of Kings.

"I'm on my way to Boss's now," Shadow said. "What the fuck's going on?"

"They lured Killian away. He got a call just before everything went black. No one's heard from Boss."

"These fuckers think they're smart. They're going to beg me to kill them when I'm through."

"I'll be there with Viper in ten."

He hung up and called Chains. Now he had to worry about Killian, too. He'd always been good at keeping his distance from everyone, never getting too close. Unfortunately, he'd formed a friendship with the Irish assassin, and his resolve to take down these assholes was even stronger.

"You hear about Boss?"

"No, what happened?" asked Chains.

"Maurice said there's a code black. It's not good. What are we dealing with, Chains? You were on the inside when I was doing intel."

"The mark was a puppet master, a big player in the underground. Now that he's gone, there's a void to fill, and more than one ready to kill to fill it."

"And Boss?"

"He's a huge threat. Killer of Kings has an iron-clad reputation," said Chains. "I just can't believe anyone had the balls to take him on."

"Where's that piece of shit you were chauffeuring around?"

There was a brief silence. "El Diablo disappeared a couple days ago. I thought we could trust him, but in this game, money's everything."

Money wasn't everything to Shadow. He'd trade it all for a normal life, a childhood he could look back on fondly. As an adult, he valued loyalty above the almighty dollar.

"I'll be at Boss's in a few minutes. Bain and Viper are on their way."

He turned off his headlights as he approached the mansion, tall decorative iron gates surrounding the entire property. Accent lighting cut the blackness at regular intervals around the perimeter, but it was still a mix of shadows. All week he'd been losing sleep protecting Riley. Meanwhile, the threat planned to attack the head of the organization, ignoring the limbs. With Killian, Boss's personal bodyguard, MIA, Boss would be alone against any number of trained killers.

He hoped they weren't too late. The leader of Killer of Kings could be dead, already at another location, or currently being interrogated. Shadow wanted to rush in with guns blazing like Killian would, but he needed to come out of this alive. Needed to return to Riley.

He got out of his car and walked down the street with his gun at his side. The light rain annoyed him, moistening his hair and getting in his eyes.

When he neared the entrance, two dark shadows waited for him.

"You hear anything?" he asked.

Viper had a black hood on, concealing his face, and Bain was openly strapped with so much fucking firepower he could take out a small army. Both men looked ready for business. For them, for Shadow, their lives revolved around death and destruction. Boss had trained most of them one on one. Whoever infiltrated Killer of Kings was in for a world of hurt.

"Nothing. It's too damn quiet if you ask me," said Viper. "I've been here before with Pepper, so I have an idea of the general main floor layout."

"So we get our asses inside, no?" Bain was a huge fucker, his ink climbing up his neck. He'd been friends with Viper since they were kids.

"There's a massive foyer beyond the doors," said Shadow. "I have the codes for the security system."

"I'm going in," said Viper. "Cover me."

Shadow entered the code into the control panel, unlocking the double front doors. Viper kicked them open, two handguns outstretched in front of him. An alarm whined every few seconds, a few emergency lights flashing red. Shadow moved to the right, Bain to the left. They swept the foyer, then spread out through the main floor.

A while later they all met up in the lobby again. A figure stood in the doorway, they all pointed their weapons.

"Hey, it's just me!" said Chains.

Shadow dropped his gun to his side and exhaled. There was no sign of Boss, no sign of a struggle. They still had to check the basement and second floor. Now there were four of them, so they had better odds.

"I'll check downstairs," said Bain after peering over the wooden banister. He pulled up an AR15, holding it chose to his chest as he descended into the basement. Shadow looked up to the second level, nodding to Viper and Chains to follow him. Within ten minutes, they'd cleared the entire house, and it was no small task. Boss obviously liked the finer things in life, and for a man living alone, he had a lot of damn rooms.

They wandered around the main floor, trying to decide on their next move.

"Does anyone know how to turn off the fucking alarm?" said Chains. The constant grating sound kept the sense of urgency at the surface.

Viper pointed out the kitchen window. There was a large pool house in the near distance, bigger than Shadow's house. They all moved without speaking, passing the massive infinity pool that overlooked a forested valley.

Bain kicked open the door, the crash shattering the silence, wood splinting inwards. Immediately, the familiar scent of blood caught Shadow's attention. The moonlight reflected off the blood pooling on the floor, the dark crimson liquid the only witness to whatever the fuck killed Boss.

"Check the lights," said Shadow. When the overhead lighting snapped on, the body swinging from the rafters, draining out on the tile was a morbid sight. There were other rooms, so he started to investigate the ones to the right. He knew better than to let down his guards, even if the leader of Killer of Kings had already been taken down.

"Check it out!" he shouted after entering a large guest bedroom.

The other three men came in behind him.

"Holy shit," said Viper. "What a fucking freak show."

There were bodies everywhere, in various states of dismemberment. The floor was covered in blood, flies buzzing around the corpses. Shadow had killed a lot of men and been to countless aftermaths, but nothing compared to this.

"Someone's coming," Bain whispered, pulling out his 9mm. He leaned against the inside wall, waiting to strike. Whoever walked through the living room, passing Boss's body, was not trying to be quiet. Bain pressed a finger to his lips. The second the man appeared in the entryway, Bain had his gun pressed to his temple. "Try anything and I'll blow your fucking brains in."

"Spade?" Shadow lowered his weapon. It was one of the regular guys from Boss's west end cleaning crew. He usually didn't come up this far north. "Who the fuck called you?"

"Boss. Who else?"

"When?"

"Hour ago."

Shadow pushed past him, Bain still keeping him at gunpoint. When he reached the body handing by its ankles, Shadow spun it around to get a good look at the bloodied and beaten face.

It wasn't Boss.

"Boss called you—what did he say? Where is he?" asked Shadow.

The big boy shrugged and scratched his balls. "Said to make it spotless. The mess was contained to the pool house. He said something about not fucking up his marble floors."

It sounded like Boss all right.

"Where is he? He pulled a code black."

Spade pointed to the bedroom when Lola came in the front door, stepping over debris, dragging a mop and bucket with her. "I just clean, Shadow. Ask someone else."

Lola passed by, winking at him. "When you taking me on a date, Shadow?"

"Not going to happen, Lola. I have a woman now."

"Promise I'm better than her," she said.

"Ain't gonna happen."

"Shit, are none of you still single anymore?" she complained as she moved to the bedroom, cursing when she saw the disaster in the other room. "Spade, you need to call Mikey. This is going to take a while."

As soon as Lola mentioned a date, Shadow's thoughts immediately went to Riley. He still owed her that date he promised, and she was cuffed to a radiator.

Shadow was confused as hell. The bloodbath in the pool house was courtesy of Boss, he had no doubt about that. So where was he? Where was Killian?

Until he knew more, he'd head home, then contact Maurice and see if he'd dug up anything on their locations. At least he had hope that Boss had made it out of this alive.

They cautiously made their way back to the main house. The alarm was no longer whining, and the lights were on. Shadow had his gun at the ready. Bain moved in front.

El Diablo was in the front foyer, a bloodied knife in his hand. "I want my money," he said, tossing the knife on the tiles.

Viper and Bain rushed in, ready to bring El Diablo down. Chains approached him. "You make that mess out back?"

"What mess? Boss said I'd get paid for every head. Since there're five in my trunk, I'm here to collect."

"Where the fuck have you been?" asked Chains. "You left without a word."

"Cleaning up this guy's mess." He nodded to Shadow. "And now I'm done."

Shadow gave him the middle finger.

"Boss is MIA, so until we find him, there's no payday," said Chains.

El Diablo ran a hand through his hair, blood smears on his arm and cheek. "I saw him this afternoon. He told me where I could find the last half dozen."

"You said you had five."

"Boss wanted me to let one live, so that *pinche culero* only has gunshot wounds to the kneecaps. This Boss of yours is one twisted fuck."

Shadow couldn't stick around. He needed to get home, wanted to get home. Riley would be waking up soon, and he didn't want her to panic when she found herself bound.

"I'll contact Maurice," said Shadow. "He must have picked up something on Boss or Killian by now."

He took a breath once seated in the driver's seat of his car, calling Maurice on his cell phone.

"Maurice, did you track anything?"

"Killian's with Boss. They were at the docks an hour ago. I picked them up on the CCTV cameras," he said. "They're usually there to dump bodies."

"Well, his pool house looks worse than a slaughterhouse. Why would he call in a code black if he had things handled?" Shadow asked.

"I don't even pretend to understand that man. I can only speculate it was part of his strategy. He's only human, Shadow, like you. Maybe he just needed to know his men had his back."

"Call me once you make contact." Shadow ended the call and hit the highway.

****

Riley heard the front door open. She was beyond pissed off and ready to give Shadow a piece of her mind. When she'd woken up on the floor, unable to free herself or even stand up straight, she'd panicked until she convinced herself Shadow had to return at some point.

When he peered in the doorway, she frowned. "Why am I handcuffed? I told you I was okay with you handling your business, didn't I?"

"I know you, Riley. You're too curious for your own good. I didn't want you to get hurt."

"I wasn't going to do anything."

He bent down and unlocked the cuffs, massaging her wrist once she was free. "I'm sorry, baby. It's been a fucked-up day."

"Look, you have to trust me. How can we have a relationship without trust?"

Shadow smirked. "You're right. I'm so used to relying on myself, not trusting anyone. It's a hard way to live." He helped her to her feet, and pulled her close.

There was something in his eyes, something different, almost defeated. She didn't like it. As much as she'd love to ream him out for everything—the assassins, the cameras, the handcuffs—she couldn't. She just wanted to love him, to be the rock he needed. He'd given her a sense of security and belonging since coming into her life, so she knew how precious that feeling was.

"Things are different now," she said. "At least I hope they are."

He kissed her on the lips, just once. "I do trust you, I'm just terrified of losing you."

She cupped his cheek. "I've survived this long. You won't be able to get rid of me that easily." Then she thought about why he'd been gone in the first place. Had things gone well? Did she still need to stay cooped up or could she return to her bakery and live her life? "So, what happened? Did you find out what's going on?"

He released her waist and ran a hand through his tousled hair. "It was a mess. I need to hear from Boss himself. Until I do, we need to wait this out."

She scowled, but at least Shadow had come back to her alive. When she'd first woken up all she could think about was something terrible happening, never seeing her man again, and dying of starvation on the floor because he had the key.

"I don't know how I'm ever going to get used to this," she said. "Your life is crazier than my murder mystery books."

"How's the romance?"

Riley bit her lip. Just thinking about their emerging love life made her cheeks flush. "I guess it's better than the books." She couldn't believe she'd just said that. All her adult life, she'd convinced herself that true love didn't exist. Now she was living the dream.

Immediately, her thoughts drifted into forbidden territory. She'd never get enough of Shadow. "Did you kill anyone today?" She pushed his jacket off his strong shoulders, exposing his harnesses. One by one, she disarmed him, placing the weapons carefully on the counter.

"Not today."

She ran her nails down the front of his t-shirt, then proceeded to work on his belt. "Maybe next time," she said, focused on her task. The idea of fucking Shadow in his weapons room was an instant turn-on.

"I thought you were mad at me," he said, holding

her wrist in place before she could unzip his pants.

"Well, think of this as your chance to make it up to me."

"You're gonna regret those words." He had fire brewing in his eyes now, his concern shifting to something dark and dirty. She swallowed hard, anticipation making her entire body hum with need.

He hoisted her up onto the counter, positioning himself between her legs. Shadow tugged off her shirt and removed her bra. "I love these tits," he said, holding them up in his hands. She knew he wasn't trying to be nice. His desire was palpable, and she felt drunk on the feeling of being wanted unconditionally.

His tongue flicked her nipple before he engorged himself, sucking and licking her breasts until she was holding his hair and panting his name.

"Are you wet for me, baby? You want me to fill your tight little cunt with my cock?"

She nodded, her lust taking over, making her almost light-headed with desire. Riley loved how her big, stoic beast had such a dirty mouth during sex.

"I want to make you feel good, too," she said.

"Trust me, all you do is make me feel good." He suckled her neck, teasing her erogenous zones until her eyes lolled back in her head.

She reached between them and roughly palmed his cock. "I want your big dick. I want to feel you in my mouth."

Shadow groaned, placing his hand over hers. "You're a bad girl, Riley."

Holding his shoulders, she slipped off the counter and went down to her knees. "It's only fair. I want to know every inch of your body too." She smiled as she released his erection, a bead of pre-cum glistening on the tip. It felt empowering knowing that she was about to make a hitman beg—*her* hitman.

Chapter Twelve

Flicking the tip of Shadow's cock, Riley tasted him, wanting more. She licked along his cock, following down the vein at the side, and pulling back up to take the head of him into her mouth. She moaned around his length as she slowly sank her mouth onto his cock. When he hit the back of her throat, she looked back up at him, seeing the frown on his lips.

Pulling off his cock, she began stroking up and down. "What's wrong?"

"I don't want to come yet. Do you know how sexy it is to see your lips wrapped around my dick?"

To torment him even more, she took his cock back into his mouth, tasting him, wanting him to come because of her touch.

Shadow ran his fingers in her hair, clenching his hand into a fist to hold her head. She felt the strength of his hand as he began to pump his cock into her mouth, hitting her throat with every plunge.

Suddenly, he pulled away, shaking his head. "I want your pussy on my mouth. I want you to ride my face."

He always got what he wanted, and within a matter of seconds, he had her pants off, and he was lying on the cold, tiled floor.

"I want you to put one knee there, and another there."

She shook her head at his instruction. "No."

"I'm going to hold your hips as you ride my face. I'm not going anywhere. Come on, baby. If you loved me, you'd let me taste that pretty pussy."

Riley didn't know why she was nervous. Being a bigger woman, she didn't think about doing a sixty-nine position. She'd even recalled cruel jokes from an old boyfriend about this very thing, saying she'd suffocate him if they tried. But, she knew Shadow wouldn't budge until he got what he wanted, so even as she was nervous, she moved so that she was over his head, facing his feet.

His hands moved down the curve of her ass, and he tugged her down even more so that her pussy was directly over his face.

"You're feeling like a little virgin right now, babe," he said. "All nervous, even though you and I both know how much I love to eat out this cunt."

He spread her pussy lips, and then his tongue flicked over her clit, making her gasp, and with his touch, she completely forgot that she didn't want this.

"Suck my cock, baby."

Wrapping her fingers around the length of his dick, she covered the top, taking him into her mouth, bobbing her head up and down. More of his creamy pre-cum leaked out of the tip, and she closed her eyes, enjoying the taste of him as he slid in her mouth. He was hers, and she loved everything about him.

He ravished her pussy, licking her clit, sucking the bud into his mouth, and sliding down to plunge inside her. He'd fuck her with his tongue, only to draw back up, and tease her clit once again.

The pleasure was insane, utterly dirty, especially as he began to stroke across her anus, reminding her of how good it was to have him sliding his dick into her ass.

She began to rock her pussy onto his mouth, unable to keep still as he teased her, bringing her close and closer to orgasm with every passing second.

His cock, still rock hard, filled her mouth, and she sucked him in deep, wanting every single part of him.

She wanted him to come apart, to fill her mouth with his release so she could swallow him down, tasting him, becoming one with her man.

As she wriggled on top of him, he started to thrust his cock up, making her take more of him, and she didn't deny him.

Their licking and sucking became more frenzied as they neared climax.

Riley cried out as Shadow brought her to her peak first. The shock of her orgasm rocked her body to the very core. She took more of his cock into her mouth, her need driving her actions wild. He held her steady, prolonging her beautiful orgasm.

Slowly, he brought her down from the peak as he found his own. He thrust inside her mouth, and his cock swelled a second before his cum flooded her mouth.

Swallowing him down, she licked his cock until he shook, unable to handle anymore.

A wave of unadulterated satisfaction flooded her veins, calming her raging libido. She savored that post-orgasmic bliss.

Shadow lifted her up, and moved her so that she was straddling his legs. They were on the floor in his weapons room, but it was such an intimate moment—quiet, just the two of them. He cupped her cheek, and smiled. "I knew I could get you to be as wicked as me. You have the prettiest pussy I've ever seen, just so you know."

"You're not supposed to tease me with that."

"I can't resist." He ran his thumb across her bottom lip. "I was only half a man until I met you. I can see that now."

"It must be love." She smiled. "You're the first man to cuff me to a radiator, and get me to suck his cock all in the same day."

Shadow laughed, and she loved the sound he made. Running her hand down his chest, she began to feel a little worried.

"Do you think something bad has happened to your friends?" she asked.

"I don't know. With the mess I saw, I doubt it. I don't know why they didn't stick around though." He rubbed at his eyes, and she cupped his face this time.

"Whatever it is, we'll handle it together. I can promise you."

He smiled. "You're the love of my life, woman. Who would have thought I'd fall for a girl who likes to stalk people?"

She chuckled. "Investigate, not stalk, and I've only ever done it with you."

Seeing that he needed a distraction, she moved over his body, pushing him down to straddle his waist. His cock was still flaccid, but she knew how to get him all excited again.

"I want you to stop thinking and to focus on me."

"You've got my full attention, baby."

Taking his hands, she placed them on her breasts. She knew how much they'd both been through in life, experiencing some of the same nightmares and letdowns in their childhoods. Finding each other was a godsend, and she knew they both understood the value of having someone love them unconditionally.

"You've got me, Shadow. No matter what happens, I'll stay by your side through thick and thin. I've got your back, and I'll do everything I can to take care of you."

"You're getting all mushy on me here. What happened to my hard-ass neighbor?"

"I'm still your hard-ass neighbor. I'm just letting you know you're not alone anymore. And neither am I." She kissed his lips, and as his cock began to swell. She smiled.

The love she felt for this man surprised her at

times, but she knew their love was the kind that lasted a lifetime.

****

One week later

"You bought this?" Shadow asked, looking at Boss.

The owner of Killer of Kings didn't even have a scratch on him. Shadow had been mid-way through fucking Riley when the call came in that Boss and Killian were alive and well.

What pissed him off was the fact he didn't have a clue what the two men were doing, or why they'd gone off the grid. Boss was a mean motherfucker, and the way he'd taken out all of those men had surprised him.

Most of the time he wanted to kill Boss for his interfering ways, but when he got the code black, he'd been worried. Killer of Kings was nothing without Boss.

Every single man who worked for him was better for Boss and what he did, and Shadow didn't want to lose him.

"Of course I bought it. Not only have I done that, but I'm giving you the largest unit, rent free, Riley," Boss said.

"What?" Riley asked.

"I did speak English, didn't I?" Boss asked. "I thought you'd like this investment. I got rid of that dirty fucking bar. I like coming to this plaza, and that place ruined it for me. I happen to like your sugar cookies, Riley." He winked.

This was all news to Shadow, who simply smiled, shocked at what Boss had given Riley. It was perfect.

Boss handed her the keys. "There's a designer in the old bar waiting for you. It's a huge unit. He says he can have the bakery and shop you want within a month. Get what you want, and don't let him bulldoze you into doing what he wants."

Riley's mouth was open in shock as she took the keys, staring at them for a moment. Shadow laughed as she threw herself at Boss, and in that moment, he saw the tenderness on Boss's face, which was gone within seconds.

If he hadn't been watching, he'd have missed it.

"Go on. I don't have all fucking day."

Boss had called him that morning, and ordered him down to Riley's old bakery. Shadow never expected this, but he saw what it meant to his woman.

"She's a good one. You've got to keep the kind that can bake close. In my line of work, a chocolate pie cures all problems," Boss said.

"Are you going to tell me what went down?"

"You don't need to trouble yourself over it, Shadow. A hit on Killer of Kings was expected. I don't think they knew what they were dealing with. It was good to have my men come and help me though. That was … worth it."

"Where did you and Killian go? We were all worried."

Boss smiled, and it was a wicked smile. "We went to pay some friends a visit, Shadow. You know there're cameras inside my buildings. They record and see everything. We made sure that no one else ever gets the idea to try and take me out. I run an organization of killers who get the job done right. I don't run from threats. Never have. I stand and I fight. Let's just say anyone else who thought they could win by taking me down, they've been warned."

Shadow held his hand out to shake, and Boss took it.

Leaving the leader of the Killer of Kings, he made his way inside, and saw Riley smiling and clapping her hands. She turned when she saw him, running up and throwing herself into his arms. He laughed as he twirled her in the air.

"I love it. This is so awesome. I can't believe I don't have to worry about anything. I can have the bakery that I've always wanted. Everything I've ever dreamed of."

"You started this dream yourself, Riley. Don't forget that. And it was your hard work that paved the way. We're going to live this dream together, babe. Every single dream, we're going to do it together." He set her back on her feet. "I want you to marry me."

"What?"

"You heard me. I want us to have a life together, to put a ring on your finger, and to spend the rest of my life loving you. We'll be a real family. Hell, maybe we can be foster parents, great foster parents, and adopt kids of our own. I know how amazing you are, Riley, and I know how lucky I am that you picked me."

"I haven't agreed to marry you yet."

He slammed his lips down on hers, feeling her melt against him. "You will."

"Are you always so certain?" she asked.

Shadow ran his thumb across her lips, shaking his head. "I've only ever been certain of one thing. I can't live without you, Riley. Not now, not ever. I want to give you the world, and to wake up with you every single day."

Tears filled her eyes, and when they spilled down her cheeks, he wiped them away.

He cocked an eyebrow. "My declaration of forever was supposed to make you happy."

"It does make me happy, Shadow. So happy." She gripped his shirt, nodding her head. "Yes, I'll marry you. Yes, we can have a family, and I'd love to wake up beside you for the rest of our lives."

If they didn't have an audience, he'd have made love to her there and then, as it was, he held Riley's hand as she dealt with the guy who'd refurbish her new place.

He didn't think for a second that he'd ever get a chance to find love, or to be happy. Riley was his life now, and the future they had together was one he looked forward to sharing with her.

For now and forever, he'd love her.

The End

www.samcrescent.com

www.staceyespino.com

SAM CRESCENT & STACEY ESPINO

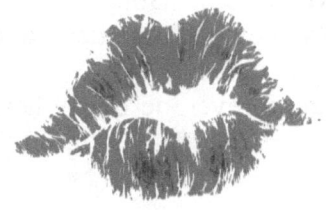

EVERNIGHT PUBLISHING ®

www.evernightpublishing.com